STAB IN THE BACK

STAB IN THE BACK

by

CHARLES DRUMMOND

WALKER AND COMPANY
New York

All the characters and events portrayed in this story are fictitious.

First published in the United States of America in 1970 by the Walker
Publishing Company, Inc.

Published simultaneously in Canada by The Ryerson Press, Toronto.

ISBN: 0-8027-5211-X

Library of Congress Catalog Card Number: 70-120403

Printed in the United States of America from type set in the United
Kingdom.

CHAPTER ONE

O F T H E T W O men seated on rickety kitchen chairs a couple of feet back from the uncurtained window, one liked to smoke and was now reduced to morosely chewing gum, the other did not smoke but drank, and the sickly stench of rum mingled with the pervading smell of old plumbing. "I wish I knew how we got this ruddy assignment." The voice was a mere croak as the speaker removed the gum and stuck it under the chair seat. He was a big man, a police sergeant of some seniority, known because of his cunning arts as 'Crying' Jarvis.

His companion, senior in years, a man stuck for ever on the sergeant's rung of the promotional ladder, did not trouble to reply. It was seven hours since they had cautiously surmounted the back fence of the old, condemned two-storey house for the sixth day running. Jarvis put his question every hour and the sergeant, Reed by name, no longer heard it properly, but it niggled him all the same. He had to think of something. Twice he had run through the score of Schumann's *Etudes Symphoniques*, a musical ear and memory being his main interest other than drink; and now he had been reduced to recapitulating the various brands of rum he had ever known. He had reached eighteen when his train of thought was interrupted.

It had started a week ago and there had been nothing much on his desk. Reed's beat was the London 'sporting' fraternity, which covered a wide area of activity. Over the years he had become an adept at faking work. You had to, really, otherwise as a low-ranking jack-of-all-trades you were likely to find a wad of thankless chores on your desk twice a day. He had been seated peaceably at his desk in the cubby-hole he shared with three other sergeants, waiting for opening time, wondering about a certain casino operator, when the red bulb flashed on the small desk intercom. This meant you dropped everything, or at least put it down. In this case it was a generous measure of brandy disguised as coffee from the Sergeant's flask.

"Oh, Sergeant, I know how busy you are. . . ." Superintendent Quant's gentle voice paused in its all too familar gambit.

"I'm just finishing something urgent, sir, then I'll be right up."

It was some years since Reed had bothered about chlorophyll tablets, but as a perfunctory gesture to rank he chewed some heavily cloved sweets before taking the lift.

Superintendent Quant was a kind of keeper of Her Majesty's Conscience, not of the monarch in person but of her ministers who answered questions both in the Commons and the Lords. He dealt with the moral implication of things, in a comfortably biblical style he had made his own, such as could be intoned by the Government understrapper concerned. What was he on to now? mused Sergeant Reed. Probably still bulls: fighting bulls. It had been suggested that the effect of indiscriminate bull-fighting upon the soil of Gibraltar would produce havoc among the moral sensibilities of the inhabitants and the crews of ships who anchored off the Rock, thereby strengthening British claim to this amalgam of kippers, bad beer, bougainvillea, gambling, short weight and currency fiddling.

Quant was finding evidence hard to get. Snivelling children, back on solid soil after a twenty-guineas-per-head tour of Spain, and remorselessly interrogated by local welfare officers, had related gory details with curious, hiccupping relish; their parents, vowing that tame stags could not drag them again to such outrages, had a glazed expression when recounting their moral rape. It could scarcely stand a Government commission. The only really forceful evidence

6

had come from a Russian trawler captain who had seen it—on TV in a Gib. chip shop—and said he was disgusted. Superintendent Quant, however, was always allergic to politically coloured evidence.

The squeaking of his old, massive barrelled fountain pen had been the only sound as Reed tapped and entered the cosy, rosewood room which was the reward for the Super's public servitude and years of never having made a wrong decision by dint of making virtually no decisions at all. Quant knew all the tricks, all the angles, was not unpleasant for the sake of being so, and Sergeant Reed rather valued him.

"There is a certain house we want watched very carefully, Mr Reed," he said after the Sergeant had seated himself; "during the hours of four in the afternoon until two next morning, seven nights a week. It is of vital importance that this is done well. No lights, no smoking, no transistor radios, just sitting in a dirty little room watching through a window."

"I suppose one can think."

"Many a time I used to run through the Old Testament in my mind," agreed Quant. "It is amazing the bits you forget when it comes to the point, or the new things you discover. Not a single mention of cats, for instance, not in the New Testament either." The Superintendent's eyes had lit up. Bible study was one of the few things which could triumph over his habitual dyspepsia.

"I seem to remember things howling in the wilderness."

"Not cats," said Quant firmly. "I checked it with a bishop. Well, you'll be credited with liberal overtime to be added to your annual leave. And I can pretty well guarantee you a week's delegation to a conference on the Isle of Man. That's fixed."

Wise in the ways of Quant, the Sergeant had got up, and he was on his way to the door when the Superintendent said, absently, "Mr Jarvis will be with you. You had better brief him."

7

As Reed had expected, there was a file deposited on his battered little desk by the time he reached it.

"The old bleeder is up to his old games, I see," said a colleague, glancing up from his scrutiny of that week's classified newspaper advertisements. "Funny how smart these old procurers think themselves," he said suddenly, making a note in shorthand of an advertisement for a broad-minded secretary to work in Maida Vale.

In a way old Quant was a procurer, thought Reed, snapping the elastic off the file to reveal two stapled quarto sheets plus a carbon. At the moment it was the revival of old ambition: after years as a port captain, Quant had seen a glimpse of higher command, leading to Lord knows what in the way of superior pension, perhaps even a knighthood, or, as an outside shot, a life peerage and peaceable years spent at eight guineas per working day defending the cause of law and order. To reduce the possibility of traceable error, subordinates were called in, very vaguely briefed, and returned to their offices to find what Quant had styled "a definitive briefing"—not directly attributable to him but compiled by a subordinate—on their desks.

Reed took a swig of brandy and telephoned Sergeant Jarvis. The latter was a teetotaller and Reed had no illusions as to why he had been so paired. Jarvis was a hardworking man who liked overtime and was something of an authority on expense sheets. He did not volunteer more than necessary—Reed increasingly recognised the tendency in himself—and when not working was usually found sipping a fruit juice in the canteen. Reed eventually located him and took the lift up.

"I've got the screws this morning," said Jarvis in greeting, "a sure sign of a hot, sweaty summer ahead."

Reed plodded away and got a plastic cup of coffee, tipping brandy into it. Jarvis sniffed disapprovingly.

"A Quant briefing," said Reed, "masses of overtime. You and me. I would say reasonable expenses would not be

8

queried." He passed over the carbon copy as Jarvis licked his lips. "You know just as much as me."

The briefing read:

Re. Surveillance of 'Larchmont,' 30 Sentinal Road, N.6. between the hours of 4 p.m. and 2 a.m., this is to take place as from today until further orders.

Officers will be Sergeants Reed and Jarvis.

Method: from the front room of Number 85, Sentinal Road, one of a deserted series of row houses opposite. Permission has been obtained from the local council, the owners. The chairs have been provided. There is a lavatory flush which must be used with caution. There must be no smoking, illumination or radio. Entrance is over a back fence. (But consult Sergeant Butcher of the Division.)

It is desired that this should be regarded as 1A Classified. Sergeant Butcher or his designated deputy should be the sole local contact.

The owner and occupier of Larchmont, a four-storied detached dwelling, is a Mrs Hezekiah Cream (the Mrs is by courtesy) aged 89 years. She is in full possession of her faculties. From 9 a.m. until 6 p.m. she is attended by a Miss Birch, a lady companion, and a housekeeper named Mrs Rumming.

The object of this surveillance is to ascertain if a *general gathering of persons* takes place at Larchmont. The arrival of more than three persons—apart from the two staff ladies—at the premises and their admission must be notified to Central Switchboard, Emergency 608.

Method: Proceed over back fence to the public callbox marked on the accompanying sketch.

Note: We may be up against sharp brains and resource.

Reed, who could encompass whole paragraphs with his bloodshot eyes, went to get more coffee as Jarvis, using a

9

knife as a ruler under each line absorbed the wisdom contained on the pages.

"Ever known one quite like this, Mr Reed?" he said eventually.

Reed shrugged. "Perhaps blackmail," he said, "and on an important scale. I think, friend, the less we know the better. Have no mercy with the exes."

"Taking your car?"

On night jobs Reed often drove Jarvis home in his new Aston Martin D.B.S. : an inbuilt censor prevented him from taking the wheel when drunk. Such an arrangement sometimes meant several pounds per week in Jarvis's pocket : in return he protected Reed, as did quite a number of people, when the Sergeant achieved the blind staggers or lost control of his bladder.

"I don't think I like it," said Jarvis, the corners of his mouth creeping down.

"I'll get the wife to cut sandwiches," said Reed. "We can put in for a packed hamper." Jarvis brightened.

"I do not like it, Mr Quant," the Deputy Commander a red-faced man of deceptive amiability, had said a day previously. "I do not want to prejudice you, but there is a smell of old drains about this. Anyway let's go to the small conference room." The D.C. had given Quant lunch at his club, a troublesome business entailing a word with the steward and totally bland food. The Superintendent never appeared to realise what trouble the nervousness and rumbling of his intestines occasioned other people. The D.C.'s own digestion, inured like a thoroughbred engine to high-octane feeding, had not appreciated the meal. Thank God it was one of the better clubs, thought the D.C., where

Quant's request for barley water had passed reasonably unnoticed.

The conference consisted of five depressed policemen and a rubicund civilian from the Treasury.

"The case," said the D.C., as the tape recorder flashed on its red light, "concerns the Sixteenth Baron Dockern who with his wife and staff of three were killed when their home, 'Briar Heights', was destroyed by enemy action in 1941. His Lordship was fifty, a member of a merchant bank. They had one son who predeceased them by three weeks in the Western Desert. Lord Dockern had succeeded his father, a retired Brigadier turned city gent, in 1938. In 1941 the family came to an end, what money there was—a total of some two hundred thousand pounds—going through the remote distaff side to people in Rhodesia. These people can be, I consider, dismissed.

"The Dockern fortunes date from the late seventeenth century when a younger son of a Northumberland family came to London and became liked by William the Third, that unattractive monarch, and his wife Mary. They found him an heiress and a barony, he bought land in Suffolk and built Briar Heights. In 1941 it was a baggy-looking old house, of forty-five rooms, standing in eight acres. The Dockerns were not sentimental, and the old farms had long since been developed for building. I must try to give you a little background"—the Commander, himself only preserved from a penurious peerage by two elder, childless brothers, clasped his hands behind his head. "After the first flurry, they made no great splash. An admiral here, an administrator there, younger sons governing the unfortunate Australians, that sort of thing. But there was a solid core of accountancy. The Enclosures, the Industrial Revolution, the rape of the Highlands, the exploitation of India, all required capital. It did not grow on trees, as some historians would lead state-educated children to believe, but was provided by people like the Dockerns. Under the ermine robes lurked a perfectly good, for those days, chartered accountant. They waxed fat: in the nineteenth century they discovered the City, banking, insurance, joint stock swindles, and even mutual funds. I must now ask our friend, uh . . ."

The staff of the Treasury, who see people at their worst, are for some reason jolly, even the quiet ones who play chess a lot. That day's representative was chuckling to himself. "Admirable, Commander, admirable indeed. You must, uh, forgive me if I point out the obvious, but it has been only recently in our system that paper has been accepted. Totally unbacked paper! I remember playing bezique with my dear mother and using million mark notes and paper roubles for counters, she not approving of gambling for money. And the franc of course, and the peseta notes which actually disintegrated! Dear me! So, of course, people always like *things*. And there was a streak in the original Dockern! Mind you, how near he was to the days when the King could take the lot off you! And if he didn't there was the Church!" Always sensitive to atmosphere, the Treasury representative noticed Quant's jowls register outrage. "I refer to the days before the Great Statute, gentlemen, before *Praemunire* protected John Citizen in our modern democratic way," he intoned smoothly. "But there was an early tradition of 'the Dockern Treasure', because any looter, indiaman captain, or freebooter could always sell precious stones to the Dockerns, who paid in gold and silver coins. In turn the Dockerns took good care to garner as much hard cash as possible. It is of course the ideal situation from a, um, fiduciary viewpoint. Why," he was warming to his task, "they work like hell to amass a little ready money, shrewdly invest it as they think right, and, then, ahum. . . . God and economics work in mysterious ways, gentlemen. It did not really matter until the last century. Before that, to put it crudely, they ripped it off you when they wanted it and Parliament was against it. But of course the form gradually reversed itself. The Dockerns in the nineteenth century paid very few taxes. Even Mr Gladstone made one of his famous calculations concerning a family who owned property worth two million pounds who paid income tax, at the rate of sixpence in the pound in those days, upon three hundred and twenty-four pounds and ninepence, representing a church living which for spiritual reasons they could not conceal. The House of Commons was convulsed with laughter."

He could have governed Australia if he had been born a couple of steps up, ruminated the D.C.; that was before they put natives into the job—and a good thing too— although he seriously doubted whether the worries would have been worse, though they said that the strong grog and tough meat played hell at times. He cleared his throat. "What you are saying, sir, is that the Dockerns kept their money in jewellery."

"That is so. When death duty began, surprisingly little came from their estate. The family gradually died out, and the money pertaining to cadet branches became thinly spread, but the essential oak tree always had a male heir until its extinction in 1941. In the eighteen-seventies there was heavy Dockern buying, sir, a lot of gems coming on the market from France and Italy at that juncture. There was a death in 1893, one in 1900, and another in 1920. By that time it had hotted up, and Caesar's share from them was woefully light. Fiddling! In 1918 there were rare pickings in the gem market from Russia—whole collections. In fact these are the main motivating factors. Should we return them, the Russians will lock them into vaults along with all the Cezannes, inspect them via Party auditors once a year, but also redeem a great number of Estonian bonds held by British investors, by which token a great improvement in international relations will take place."

The man from the Treasury paused, seeing alarm in the faces before him, experiencing silence except a faint, protesting colonic groan from Quant. But one was so jolly back in the office that one forgot how morose they grew in the lesser branches of public service! Oh, well, here was the time for the dramatic punch line. "It might, you know, be a matter of twenty-five million."

He noted that it made them sit up, but if anything their expressions depressed. "We have to take into account certain movements in paper currency," he said carefully—never, his first chief had impressed, does a Treasury man express a definite opinion: that was politician's pigeon. "But our experts think the figure quoted is possibly not too high. A lot of the old gems would be badly cut, of course, but on the other hand, during the Barnato Rhodes duellings a great many uncut stones were acquired very cheaply by the Twelfth Baron." He paused. "In 1939, one month before the, er, declarations of war by various people"—never admit we had anything to do with it, had said his trainer—"the Treasury was approached by Messrs Podling and Podling, of Crumpiton Magnus, Suffolk, solicitors for the fifteenth Baron. An old-established, honourable firm, they placed before us a hypothetical question. Suppose a certain family possessed a store of jewels, never assessed for death duty, worth in the nature of six million pounds. Sixty per cent of the corpus might have been acquired before 1895, the rest between that date and 1919. What would we settle for?" He shrugged. "In those days, gentlemen, it was possible to have a settlement. This is not official, nor should it be quoted, but we might have been satisfied with four million in full settlement, cash or kind. We cannot," he rolled his gooseberry eyes to the sound-proofed ceiling, "visit the sins of the fathers; or at any rate we didn't then."

"Six million pounds' worth of loot in 1939 would be worth twenty-five million today. Is that what you are saying?" asked the D.C. His own family fortunes, based on Bristol slavers, had been largely gulped by death duties and a predilection for brandy and early death on the part of the donors of fixed trusts.

"Quite."

14

"And the surmise is that the jewels were concealed in the ancestral home, Briar Heights?"

"Indeed, Commander. When war broke out, the Dockern-Podling file was labelled 'Pending Investigation'. The solicitors were notified to that effect. In due course the Dockerns were killed. We have no doubt that an exhaustive search was made by the then Mr George Podling. No assets other than property, securities and current balances existed : probate was granted in 1945, by mutual arrangement. One may say that the Treasury can admit no variation, or, perhaps one might say deviation from procedure as stipulated departmentally within the then ministerially received guide lines."

The little bastard was invoking the protective spirit of Winston Churchill, thought the D.C. Or was he concerned then? Stafford Cripps perhaps? It all seemed a very long time ago.

"Was there an F-notice?" An elderly chief superintendent, on the D.C.'s immediate left, raised his head.

"I'm afraid . . ."

"I was in charge of a bit of that. F-notices they were known as in Civil Defence. We used to translate it as 'there might be something effing queer here, Percy'. It meant heavy duty sifting. Sometimes it was some smart gent murdering his wife the instant the old house started to collapse, sometimes probate, once the home of the biggest fence in west London. Was there an F-notice regarding Briar Heights?"

The man from the Treasury was delving into a file. "Yes," he said, "though it was two weeks until it percolated through. I see they searched in 1941 and again in 1945."

"They'd have sieved everything," said the Chief Super. "If there was anything to be found, they've found it, or else it got blown to hell."

"The only thing is," said the D.C., thinking dolefully of the endless conferences likely to arise out of this business, "it might well not have been. We must keep it in our heads that the stones were almost entirely unset. A few pieces of considerable importance were not, but the majority were unset and the whole lot could be fitted into a suitcase between lashings of cotton wool, or so my expert report has it. Nine months ago a man called Fatty Fish, a high-class operator, was picked up in Miami. He's a kind of Cuban himself. It is not on record that he is a receiver of stolen goods, but he is a wheeler-dealer and an acknowledged expert on jewellery. The American Customs found him with a swag of stuff, not, so far as can be ascertained, stolen, but with no Customs' invoices to establish its legal presence. There was one piece known as Abbot Chrysthem's Gyve, not the antique dance, but the ancient shackle. He was a Welsh abbot. In approximately 1102 a knight called in, back from the First Crusade. He had a holy relic obtained at the fall of Antioch. The Abbot accused him of heresy and the fellow was burned. The relic was a largish bracelet, and when the good Abbot put it on, it refused to come off, growing tighter and tighter until he turned black and died. It is of gold, softish, nine inches in circumference, with two rubies set into spinel and peridot. Its boiling down value would be about one hundred pounds. As for an auction, well what would King Solomon's mummified remains make today? I saw an 1890 commode fetch eighty-seven pounds the other day. The point about the Gyve is that it may well have been the earliest symbol of authority among the early Christians—Antioch is where they took the name itself. The Museum says that if all is kosher they would, if allowed, start bidding around ninety thousand, with no expectancy of getting on target until double that."

"They would *not* be allowed," said the man from the Treasury, polishing his glasses.

He'd be about thirty-two, thought the D.C. Brainy, of course, as you had to be to have his job. An infant when Briar Heights went up.

"Whatever its provenance," said the D.C., "this bauble lay around for a long time. It represented an unsavoury bit of ecclesiastical history and the church did not publicise it: Cromwell's men couldn't get a boiling-down price from the local puritan fence: it was worn by a parochial beadle at one stage and the First Baron Dockern acquired it for eight and sixpence, a year's wage for a farm labourer at the time."

"Could the Miami job be a fake?" somebody asked.

"No. The Dockerns were close-mouthed about the jewellery, but they could not be wholly that about the historical bits. It was measured, photographed, and was on display on three occasions."

"Let me get this straight," said a smallish inspector with straight black hair, a man who knew every alleyway of the City of London and the scandals of many a boardroom on them, "would they not have sold bits off from time to time, that being the purpose of the exercise?"

"I think I may answer that," said the man from the Treasury, "because the late Mr Podling made it clear. The Dockern Treasure represented money hived off and frozen. Dowries, younger sons, charities, etcetera were adequately met from income: once the trap snapped on a gemstone, there it remained."

"There was that letter from the Diamond Syndicate," said an inspector who appraised gems. "I thought at the time they were proposing to donate large sums to various local charities! But when you really examined it they seemed to be exercised by various 'unmonitored stones' being sold, about as vague as you can get. The period is the last fifteen years."

"Much?" said the D.C.

"Oh, they seemed to reckon that there *might possibly* be seventy thousand pounds worth of very high quality stuff coming on the London market during that period. A flea-bite, you might say, but big fleas don't think smaller ones should have teeth."

"I suppose there's not much to be done," said the D.C.

The Inspector shrugged. "An experienced man can tell a lot from a stone, but there are a *lot* of stones. Dealing is often done by a simple form of memo, but the trade is very sensitive, particularly in the very high-grade market."

The Deputy Commander said: "There is something I want very clearly established. Intrusion by the Inland Revenue is an area of considerable public sensitivity. Any suggestion that the police were aiding . . ." He paused, conscious of the fact that his mind was ahead of his tongue.

"Oh, I'll accept *vultures*," said the Treasury representative at his jolliest. The D.C. noticed with dislike that the man wore a Harrow tie.

"Aiding the process of tax collection would cause a public outcry. A false one. As you know we do not normally solicit or give information to other government agencies unless some specific crime is involved. This is on our files as the suspected theft of jewellery and other valuables the property of the late Lord Dockern."

"Who would get the pelf if we recover?" asked somebody.

"Oh, my master would give it to the deserving poor, you know him." Perhaps they could be a bit jolly at that, thought the Treasury man.

"More likely spend it on drawing up plans for an aircraft that never gets built."

"Now," said Superintendent Quant, with his valuable talent for the obvious, "who nicked it?"

"Evacuees, " said the D.C.

"Oh, my God," said the inspector who specialised in City affairs.

"In the January of 1940 six children named Cream were evacuated to Briar Heights. They were: Peter Cream, aged thirteen; Joan Cream, aged eleven; Ambrose Cream, aged ten; Dick Cream, eight, and twins, Giles and Sally, aged six. There were various kinds of dispersals: a very sad sight it was on the railway station which some of you younger chaps may not remember. The Cream children went, as far as records have it, by private arrangement between Lord and Lady Dockern and the grandmother of the children, a certain Hezekiah Cream, of Larchmont, Sentinal Road, N.6. It was a large brood for those days. The parents were a happy-go-lucky pair of fourth-rate music hall entertainers who stayed at Larchmont when resting. In 1938 they had a summer engagement with a beach concert party at Margate. It came to an end in the September, and there was the usual booze-up at a pub. The Creams decided to walk home and fell over the North Foreland. Autopsy registered that they were both drunk. Nothing vicious : the season's end, a wake by people who would probably never meet again. They were a popular couple, he thirty-three, she a year younger. The grandma is something else again, a retired courtesan surnamed Jones. I use the term advisedly. She was at her peak just before Victoria died, and she retired in 1926, on an annuity of twenty-five pounds a week—a lot in those days—and a seventy-eight year lease of Larchmont. She was theoretically an actress. French window stuff, the family assembled looking out into the garden, through which somebody appears. She just sat and looked beautiful for five quid a week as one of the daughters. As you know, or if you don't you are all senior enough to know, we have a filing system dealing with the sexual habits of everybody in public life. It goes back to 1873. Nobody may consult it without written permission from the Home Secretary, who is himself precluded from ever consulting it. The facts are fed in as they come to the notice of various officials, and the cards are marked up by a confidential official who is sworn to his duty.

"I suppose it was the twenty-five million," the D.C. remarked, "but I got permission." He sat for a moment remembering the overheated, long room, and the totally bald, sallow man in an alpaca jacket. "She never made the

top league, but practised steadily in division two. Four
princes of dynasties that frankly I have never heard of, a
Minister of Health, a couple of then famous American finan-
ciers, a French General (I must say that reading the annotation, it was no wonder his troops eventually mutinied) and
a lot of the squirearchy trying out London. A witty woman,
sometimes seen at the Café Royal giving as good as she got
in conversation. There is no sign of any Mr Cream, nor any
record of marriage or of the registration of her son."

"An offence," grunted somebody.

"But an upper or lower class offence," said the D.C.,
"not a middle class Edwardian offence. There was a Dockern, younger brother of the last Baron's father, who cropped
up in the report. Gay week-end parties, and this man was
listed as 'among those present'. He was killed on the Somme.
He might have sired the son, who had a couple of pounds a
week from an endowment policy in his own right.

"Now, to get back to the night of September twenty-first
1941, the Dockerns were home. Lord Dockern had transformed his acres into a pig farm. There were three Land
Army girls who lived in the village. Dockern had been
grabbed by the Ministry of Economic Warfare and was
being briefed for Ankara. He hoped to see his son, who was
already dead though he did not know it. The house was run
by two resident servants—both bodies were recovered—plus
a gardener who lived out. There were two daily cleaning
women. The Dockerns and the servants professed an aristo
contempt of bombs, but they looked after the Cream children.

"There was what my inventory calls a capacious wine-
cellar, with solid stone walls. The Dockerns from time to
time speculated in wines! It appears that the last Dockern,
who was of teetotal habits had sold off most of it. The back
of the cellar, which seems to have been a separate apartment with a large oak door, had been made into a dormi-
tory for the six Cream children. Ironically, more bombs fell

near Briar Heights than their London home. Most nights the kids slept down there : I dare say it was fun. When Briar Heights crashed down, they were safe, but it took forty-odd hours to tunnel in to them."

"Gawd!" said somebody.

"Dockern was a magnificent organiser. There was an emergency tank of water, enough oil to keep two lamps going for a week, and biscuits and tinned meat in a cupboard. The eldest boy, Peter, was always checked to see he had the key. They were fine. Let me play you this passage, part of a tape-recording made last week, by Henry Stryver, machine-minder, on heavy-rescue work between 1940 and 1945."

"When those old houses came down, they were like a pack of cards," said the comfortable, country voice. "Those up to a hundred years now, there always seemed to be a bit of them standing, but the real old 'uns were just rubble with a few fine things mixed in with it. See that pelmet? That's Adam, sir! I brought that bit home from what was left of Briar Heights plus some lovely bits of wood. Lovely bits, look at that table top. A dealer offered me forty quid when he came snooping round last winter, and two hundred for the pelmet if I'd give its signed history. I asked him what the hell you did with two hundred and forty quid these days— buy the old lady a dish-washer? He had to laugh himself, the sly little bugger from London that he was.

"Well, Rogers—he went to Canada—was the local warden and he told us about the kids. There were seventeen cases on our roster, that's how bad it was, and somebody screeching their head off under some bricks. It got you so that you started to shake yourself. And you'd only have to hang your coat up and the locals would pinch it, being the lot they are around here. We found the butler and the housekeeper, and then the Lord and Lady. Crushed to death they were, poor souls. Then it was pick, shovel and wheelbarrow : you daren't bulldoze. But the old house was on this quarried stone, wonderful workmanship. It took us a day and half, then we reached the cellar. I must say, being foreman, I thought of 'ysteria ahead, so we had the district nurse outside with her syringes at the ready. But there they were like a lot of little soldiers. They'd heard us, of course, and were neatly packed up, even the two six-year-olds holding a liddle suitcase each. They marched out and we took them to hospital, not because they were injured but for somewhere to go. I heard they went back to London three days after with their old gran."

The D.C. flicked over a switch.

"Do you mean," said Quant, "that the explosion had burst open a secret vault or something of that nature, and that these children . . ."

His wattles flushed at the thought of such depravity.

"Peter Cream!" said the D.C.

"The racing driver," said the old Chief Superintendent from the corner.

"He died ten years ago, aged thirty-three," said the D.C. "He was more than a driver, a brilliant engineer, designer and—this is interesting—as good a mechanic as you'd find. The white hope of our car industry in his time. He used to build racing cars as an experimental side-line. One went out of control about 80 m.p.h. He was a dare-devil who would probably have bought it eventually. Take a very gifted thirteen-year-old boy with time on his hands, and perhaps a mechanical puzzle such as a locked door . . ."

"The Creams!" said Quant. It was a name to conjure with. He had a slight weakness for the gossip columns and though he regarded the theatre as immoral, and the concert hall similarly except for oratorio and brass bands, he knew that Sally, Giles and Dick were straight theatre, Dick producing, and that Ambrose and Joan were impresarios of music. A talented, witty family, thought Quant, and, to the journalistic eye, united.

"I suppose there are in-laws?" he asked.

"None of the surviving five is currently married. Between

them they have fourteen 'exes' and six children. Peter was a queer. Now I suppose it is no good asking you, sir, about their income tax returns!"

The Treasury representative shook his head demurely.

"We give, you take," said the D.C., but without real hope. "Ah, well, it's back to the file of intelligent assessment. On leaving grammar schools the Creams had higher education. Oh, it's done by grants as we know, but if you have money you can do a little better. I got our universities bloke to fag round for a few days. Peter was peculiarly obtuse about some kind of maths: he engaged a private coach and worked like a dog. When he got his degree he did fifteen months as a post-grad in Sweden, at his own expense. Sally could act but had voice trouble. She employed the best doctor for her pipes plus the best coach in Europe. Now she has about the finest voice in the business.

"I had lunch with old Connor who has been on the business end of the entertainment world, oh, since Henry Ainley's time. There simply isn't anything he hasn't heard. The Creams have always been 'damn yer eyes' financially. You know the scene. The money-man wags his head and a Cream drawls, 'oh, if there's a gap of fifteen thou' we can find it'; whereupon the money-man falls over himself signing cheques. But it isn't bluff, the money-men can spot that. So there is this credibility gap between them and their capital."

"Gifts to the grannie from a potentate." Superintendent Quant's grannie had been fond of the red-jacketed magazines wherein presumably insane mill-girls refused a hundred thousand pounds from lustful and much-turbanned gentlemen from Asia.

Quant had been on dirty films and books, the D.C. remembered, but never on active vice. "The potentates were likely to settle for a sixty-five pound diamond bracelet, which the ladies used to sell back to the shop next day for forty pounds," he said. "It was considered respectable."

"Still!" Quant was doing rapid, thrifty Scotch calculations on his scratch pad. Unless he took a firm rein, realised the D.C., the whole project would bog down in discussion of the earnings of nineteenth-century courtesans. The Treasury representative had taken out his ballpoint.

"I am quite satisfied," snarled the D.C., "that Mrs Hezekiah Cream owns the unexpired lease of thirty years on her house. You might get four thousand, five hundred pounds from the people who own the ground. It's not yet on the development schedule. Everybody's waiting until the old leases are fifteen years nearer expiry. Additionally she has twenty-five pounds per week and the old age.

"I am as certain as I am sitting here that the young Creams walked away with the treasure. Firstly, they were all of very high I.Q.; secondly—and this is just based on an old annotation in a working log by somebody who died fifteen years ago—they were on their way to being juvenile gang leaders in N.6, the older ones anyway, Peter, Joan and Ambrose, three little hellions, as far as hell was available in suburbia in 1939. I suppose transference to the country," said the D.C. who glimpsed it occasionally through a car window, "quietened their propensities."

"More likely made them a damn sight worse," said the elderly Chief Superintendent, who had passed his boyhood in Devizes, Wiltshire. "Have you seen the Assize list recently? Sexual offences, strings of them!"

"I dare say country folk are full-blooded," said the D.C. as it were wrestling with the driving wheel, "but the Creams are now faced with a business decision involving ten million pounds."

"Can I borrow ten bob until Friday?" asked the Chief Superintendent.

"I think you might have better hope of borrowing ten million," said the Treasury representative.

The City Inspector took over. "It is all right. There is a tendency to entertainment conglomerates. The undertaking you refer to is a European one and comprises TV and

24

film-making, the leases or freeholds of theatres, book publishing and three concert halls. It is impossible to tell how much money the Creams will put in. It is a Swiss company. The Creams will be granted a certain number of shares in return for services rendered, and they will receive handsome salaries as artistic directors. As long as the money, or most of it, comes to London, there seems no objection."

"The Creams," said the D.C., "have that instinct to get bigger which some people have. As for me, a cottage an' a bit of rough shooting is what I dream about."

And seclusion from his wife and three unmarried daughters, thought Quant, not without charity.

"But the Creams must be the top bricks of the chimney," said the D.C. "At that I am told their artistic integrity is formidable. That Ibsen film of four years ago—a landmark one understands! But they shot, and reshot, and cut and finally took the entire bloody thing again. Old Connor says they lost, and lost very heavily rather than sacrifice perfection. A first-class impresario will do exactly that, though he must not do it often! Now, the supposition is that the treasure was taken back to the grandmother's house, hidden in the children's suitcases. And that there it remained, except for the dribs and drabs, twenty thousand here, fifty thousand there. Good God!" He paused, aghast at the sums involved.

"I think I follow your reasoning, Commander," said the City Inspector. "I adore my old mother, but I would not trust her with twenty-five million, though I must admit that my beat hardly conduces trust. So I suppose, Peter, the mechanical genius, devised a repository."

"When he was dying," said the D.C., "his brothers and sisters were scattered. The nearest was Sally who was trying something out in Edinburgh. Peter repeatedly asked that his keys—they were attached to the belt he was wearing—be sent personally to his brother, Ambrose. It is on the list taken of his effects. The usual latch and car keys, plus a key to a very good Chubb lock."

Quant, doodling, remembered that the elderly Chief Superintendent was a highly qualified engineer who headed, among other things, Explosives.

"Man can right anything he's done," said the Chief, "apart from children and hydrogen explosions. No safe or strong room exists which I could not open *if practicable*. But you can very easily make a wall-safe opened with, oh, we'll say six keys which I believe is in your mind, that explodes if tampered with. You can open it, perhaps in three-quarters of an hour, but you blow your head off. The reason they are not used is (*a*) use of a mantrap intentionally causing death renders the owner liable to a murder charge : (*b*) destruction of the contents of the safe. I could do it, if you evacuated the street and gave me a couple of truck loads of long range equipment. If Peter was that good. . ."—he shrugged—"and there was plenty of explosive around at that time. An ingenious, unscrupulous, dedicated lad . . ."

"There was an explosives store near Briar Heights, where they were evacuated," said the D.C. "The contents were meant to be used by the Home Guards to destroy bridges across a canal. The War Office Inspector marked it unsatisfactory from the security point of view in 1942. It was a cave in a hillside.

"Since we received this information we have set in motion the most systematic research programme into private safes and vaults rented out commercially as has ever been undertaken. Multiple-keyed units occasionally exist, but they are rare. We are satisfied that as far as this country is concerned, the Creams possess no such thing. Therefore, if they are liquidating a great part of the spoils, it will be taken from Larchmont over the next few weeks, and transferred to Switzerland. Presumably all the 'heirs' will foregather at Larchmont to attend to the opening of the depository."

"A Cream first night," chuckled the old Chief Superintendent. Quant realised the man's essential worldliness and sucked in his lips.

"Could we not," said Quant primly, "apply for a search warrant?"

The D.C. valued Quant. There was really nobody available who had the same mixture of knowledge, probity and non-conformist eloquence, but he did wish the man would not carry it too far.

"There is not sufficient evidence," he said carefully. "The house is owned by Grandma, who may have ancient friends with administrative teeth; the young Creams are intellectual aristocrats, and the public would not welcome the suggestion of our branch being used to collect revenue, except the proceeds of theft, smuggling, etcetera."

He looked around. Disregarding the eupeptic, scrubbed face of the Treasury representative—the D.C. remembered that the fellow wrote comic verse for *Punch* and the *New Statesman*—the dismal faces around him could be considered, in their various ways, the best implements that the nation could provide. He cleared his throat and said, "I will set up a steering committee, if you please, of you gentlemen. But I appoint Superintendent Quant in charge of the day-to-day-running of the operation, which consists of surveillance of the five young Creams. If they foregather at Larchmont it will be in the evening. I have a schedule of their activities: it is unlikely—and we have taken the risk of planting informers on a very low level—that they can go from their normal pursuits until around six o'clock. They are, perhaps significantly, rehearsing but not engaged in active production."

"If your investigations arrive at the point where you have concrete evidence, my Master will be four-square behind you," said the Treasury representative.

"Did you say 'four flushing'?" asked the D.C.

The Treasury representative gave his hearty laugh and took up his hat and brief-case. "And as we understand each other, I will leave you on this jocular note, sir." He bowed, and beamed himself to and through the door.

"Leaving us firmly carrying the pot," said the old Chief Super as it closed. "I wonder if there is reward money."

Avarice, thought Superintendent Quant. Avarice, combined no doubt only with gluttony. You had to be fairly straight with women if you wanted promotion.

"It was not insured," said the D.C. "You could not insure something of that nature. Nevertheless, I dare say we could expect some gratitude."

"We can't watch 'em too close," said the Chief Super. "Not the clever lot that they are. With permission I'll send out red notices to all ports and airports. The Customs would like such a haul."

"Thank you, expedite it please. I will authorise the money and the Treasury can scream : in the circumstances they can't do much else with their teeth. Any slings and arrows I am paid to receive. Now," he tapped a file, "there is a row of 1905 houses opposite Larchmont, compulsorily acquired from the owners. The Council will let us use one of them, entrance through the back. I think we'll put two men on to it. And of course . . ."

In some ways tape recording was a damned nuisance. In the old days he would have said bluntly, "Perhaps somebody we can dump in case of public outcry." This time he said aloud, "I thought of putting Sergeant Reed in charge."

Into the small silence dropped the thought of the two inconclusive inter-departmental enquiries, the surer knowledge of the Sergeant's inebriation, personal wealth (gained, said some, from a wealthy relative's speculations in land), personal shrewdness, knowledge of firearms and violent things, and plain luck.

"Ah," said the old Chief Super, with faded eyes caressing the little perforated box which contained the microphones, "he is a shrewd and experienced man." He repeated it for the record.

"With Sergeant Jarvis as his partner," said the D.C.

"A sober, reliable man," said Superintendent Quant. This was the truth. The addendum, "not brilliant," was never said aloud : as long as you did not fetter his expenses, Jarvis was content if need be to work out his years to the pension anywhere.

The City Inspector watched the tiny light beside the mike die out as the D.C. slid back the button.

"I sometimes wonder why Sergeant Reed stays on," he said.

It was partly the thrill of the hunt, thought Reed days later, partly because it got him out of the flat all day and partly because publicans generally gave preferential treatment to policemen even though legally it was an offence called 'harbouring'.

He looked at the glimmering dial of his watch. Five minutes to 1 a.m. Opposite, the black bulk of Larchmont was to be sensed rather than seen beyond a lamp standard unsatisfactorily placed for watching purposes. On the first floor a window became alive with light : a hell of a wattage, registered Reed. A man seemed to be clawing at the window. You could see the long, narrow distressed face and the 'O' of a panting mouth. He collapsed and slid down below the lintel as Reed sucked the remainder of his half bottle of rum.

"Get over there. Orders!" Reed made the decision automatically, as he dropped the bottle and turned on the torch clasped to the top of his raincoat. The stairs, long uncarpeted, groaned as he made a careful way down. He had forgotten about the front door, only the back being used by him and Jarvis.

"Let me," said his partner, the handier of the two, producing a flat wallet containing the essential tools. The six-inch jemmy was in segments which almost flew together in Jarvis' able hands.

"Screwed down outside," said Jervis, as he pried and levered. The door crunched and opened. "Bloody front gate'll be wired shut," said the Sergeant, but vaulted over its rusty ironwork. Shorter legged, out of breath—the rum and bacon-and-egg sandwiches playing up hellishly around his chest—Reed struggled, refused his partner's helping hand, experienced momentary panic round the crutch and alighted on the other side. A semi cul-de-sac—there were a couple of depressed side-roads and 'gardens' smelling of cats and too run down even for hardened lovers—the street was mean in a genteel way and empty. From Larchmont light still streamed from the one window like a gold-toothed smile. When they crossed the road, the two Sergeants were nearer to the house than they had ever been before. There was a gate, iron and workable, the minimum of front garden with a certain amount of greenery—not as sooty as it had probably been forty years previously, and a flight of 'area' steps leading into a basement on the one side, six steps—long ago intended for whitewash—up to the front door. Jarvis was hammering upon this as Reed puffed behind. Regulations stipulated preliminary hammering before witnesses if possible, so that a defence lawyer could not plead that electronic bells had failed.

Jarvis, a man of great physical strength which he disguised, used his feet.

"What do you think you are effing well doing?"

The door opened with alarming speed and the lady was very beautiful.

The Creams, of course, and here of all places. Sergeant Reed was a rare playgoer, but his wife liked the modern German school, and this was the theatrical Miss Sally Cream. The line came from an unsuccessful try-out at Tooting Bec, wherein a cardinal, with Sir Winston Churchill and Lord Attlee, had turned up in 1939 after a lapse of two years of improbably managing a house of ill fame financed by President Hoover.

"We have been managing a whore-house in Salerno," quoted Reed, in reply while Jarvis goggled.

She laughed and was beautiful. "Don't get fact and fiction mixed, my friend, and I *was* the more or less virginal sister-in-law. My three moral brothers are in this house and I do not autograph well after midnight." Her breath smelled a little of gin.

"You *are* a ham !" said Reed, and saw the turquoise eyes narrow a bit. "But we are officers and we think we saw somebody injured on the first floor of this building. I shall ask you to let me enter. I must warn you that it is your duty to assist the police in the execution of their duty."

"Dear God, is this the night of the long clichés?" said a male voice.

Tall, fair and blond, eyebrows knitted, registered Reed. It would be one of the family. The skin was not coarse as was normally the case with actors. He was Dick Cream, the director, the Sergeant remembered.

"You might find a long fine the end result of obstructing me," said Reed.

"Stand aside, Sally, my love. Cromwell, we have not seen our father since he quaffed yestere'en with Charles Two."

Reed saw the inside of the house was blazing with light. There was a noise of voices.

"I'm named Dick Cream," said the blond man. "Sorry and all that, but drink has been taken. A family gath, a celebration."

Reed pushed past them, conscious of Jarvis on his heels. Architecturally it was a long, narrow-gutted hallway with rooms off.

"Get upstairs and see what's happened," he said.

There seemed to be many voices, but as he came to the end room, a small but rather gorgeous late Victorian sitting-room—God knew what prices some of that stuff would

3 1

fetch—he saw that the chanting, for that was what the noise was, proceeded from a stereo hook-up to a tape recorder. A very tall, black-headed, cadaverous man reached out and flipped a switch.

"What are you doing here?" asked a small, frail, fair-haired old lady on what the Sergeant recognised as a red plush Victorian commode.

The other two occupants of the room had the blondness he associated with Creams.

"You'd be Joan and Ambrose Cream and this your grandmother? I'm police."

Ambrose Cream nodded. "And this," he indicated the tall man "is Mr Flitch. But I don't understand. Where are the others?"

"We'll sort it out," said Reed, his eyes caressing the tantalus set of grog upon the tiny table. There was a telephone, coloured red and of uncomfortable modernity, upon a shelf.

"I'll just call in headquarters." He moved forward with his deceptively light step and dialled Central Switchboard, Emergency 608.

"Larchmont, Sentinal Road, N.6," he said laconically, "It could be yellow." He used the current code for death by violence.

"What the devil is yellow?" It was Ambrose Cream, the Sergeant noticed. Of them all, he was the only one whose blondness went with a slight horsiness of bone structure and a tendency—he must be fortyish, thought Reed—of the skin to fade and dry out into unpleasant planes.

There was a nasty little silence, then Sally Cream came swiftly into the room. You always expected actors to lapse into histrionics during personal crises—the Dickensian legend—but in fact Reed, who had arrested quite a few of them, had never observed it. Sally was whitish under her light scatter of make-up, but perfectly composed. Behind her, Dick, the producer and hence more preoccupied with raw emotion, had a tic in his left cheek. Like a stout shepherd Sergeant Jarvis brought up the rear.

Old Mrs Cream got off her seat with remarkable agility and came down the two ornately carved steps leading up to it. Jarvis came in, panting.

"I suppose it's Giles," she said, making a statement. Her voice was disconcertingly young, elaborately produced, the legacy of Edwardian beauty, thought Reed.

"An accident with a spear, ma'am," said Jarvis in the curious whine he reserved for such occasions. "Quite dead, I'm afraid."

"All my progeny seem destined for violent death," said Mrs Cream, but very calmly.

"My dear"—it was Ambrose who dropped his arm around the tiny shoulders.

Jarvis had glanced at the telephone and Reed nodded affirmatively.

"The only thing at this time is a stiff drink," said the old lady. "I remember . . . I suppose you policemen will join us?"

"I'm a lifelong abstainer," said Jarvis, stung.

"Allow me to do the honours," Reed volunteered, pouncing on the tantalus and the surrounding glasses. The mahogany guard over the four decanters was unlocked. Apart from Jarvis, who abstained, and Joan Cream, who took white rum, they all had neat whisky.

"Never could stand people putting stuff in it," said the old lady regaining her seat and resting her glass on one of the broad, red plush-covered arm rests. Her head was level with that of Dick Cream, the tallest of the Creams present. Only the dark man named Flitch was a few inches above her.

"My superiors will be here, very shortly," said Reed over half a tumblerful. "Exactly where do you fit in, Mr Flitch. Excuse me, but there will be a lot of questions I'm afraid."

"Oh, I'm a United States citizen, as the accent implies. I'm a composer."

" We'll have to replace Giles," said Joan Cream. It was not callous, the way it sounded, just a plain statement of fact. "Could you get Joe? He is the best now left."

"I'll have to shuffle things around the board," said Dick, "and expensively. He's due to do a thing for Hergesheimer. If I gave Gerry Montmaster Annie Hinds for eight months—he's got that revival—then he could let Trevor have Gloria Baines for the Shakespeare bit, and Holly Oakley could go to Hergesheimer. But it will cost money."

"Hang the money," said Ambrose Cream.

"That's right, my dear," said his grandmother. "Never stint when you want a good job done."

Slyly, Sergeant Reed filled his own glass, rather wishing he had stuck to rum.

He watched Ambrose Cream put his drink down and go to the telephone and dial. The room fell silent. There was a four-minute wait. Ambrose began to talk, softly but urgently. Reed did not trouble to eavesdrop : Jarvis, always sober, was reputed to be able to hear a widow's mite drop at eighty paces on a windy day.

However, as Ambrose returned the Sergeant thought it a good idea to refill the glasses and to say, "Just for the record, Mr Cream, who was the call to?"

"Our solicitor, Mr Howe . . . he represents us all except grandmother . . . Our affairs are complicated."

Reed nodded and wandered into a corner. Howe—he had heard the name as that of a massively competent solicitor. American by origin he believed, descendant of a doyen of the New York bar of that name. He turned to look out of the window facing the back of the house, pushing aside old embroidered curtains. There was just blackness and he slid his hand further between the drapes to encounter the smooth black surface of rubber roller blinds. They used to use them in the 1939-45 war : he remembered having seen them still hanging in offices in the early fifties. He looked round the room. Impassive and utterly still, Jarvis leaned

34

against the door leading to the hall. The Creams had drawn near to their grandmother, who on her red throne looked curiously like a shrunken old judge listening to a circle of strapping young barristers. The American, Flitch, had retreated and was running back the spool in the tape recorder. He was older than he looked at first sight, perhaps forty-five.

There was a door in the corner of the room, opposite the window. Carrying his glass rather than attract attention by putting it down, Reed walked towards it, putting his feet straight up and down like a rice-field peasant. He cautiously tried the door. It opened silently outwards and he slipped through, closing it with his back. There was no light. From his breast pocket he extracted his little pencil torch, special issue and mains charged. Its brilliant ray of light shone through a clean but derelict room. There was an old bicycle leaning against one wall. Reed leaned back against the door and played the torch over it as he thought. His knowledge of these old houses—Larchmont would go back to the early eighteen-nineties he considered—was professionally thorough: useful when you had so often to search broken-down rooming houses. What was now old Mrs Cream's sanctum was probably the housekeeper's room, that uneasy but shabbily genteel roost between the servants' quarters and the gentry. There was another door ahead of him. He walked forward slowly and steadily examined it. There was a good lock. He turned the handle and opened it inwards. Moonlight streamed in. It did not look in character with the Creams to be careless about locking doors. He shrugged and stepped out into the night. It was the conventional Victorian London backyard, larger than most, in fact probably once a small garden. Access to the back door would be along the side of the house via the neat little subsidiary front gate marked 'Tradesmen', for bowler-hatted, dundrearied men in tight trousers soliciting orders, the more obsequious men selling muffins or cat's meat, or wishing to buy grease or old rags. It was a beautiful late spring night and the Sergeant stood stock still, his whisky clutched in his left hand. There was a gate at the end and he followed a little crazy-paved path to it. Almost in a dream he opened it and found himself in one of those twisted little privately-owned passages, too narrow to be designated an alleyway, which were the result of Victorian land divisions and the cause of so much trouble in later years. He walked on. It jinked sideways and, turning a narrow corner, the lights of the street ahead were visible. He did not bother to walk up to it. In his thorough way he had spent a morning cruising round the neighbourhood. The street parallel to Larchmont's own frontage comprised good-class converted flats, some new apartment buildings and professional chambers. He shrugged and retraced his steps. Originally the passages probably served half a dozen houses. Down it would go the actual deliveries, the fish, the meat, the milk and the coals. Through it maid servants had crept out on their fortnightly half-holidays.

He opened the back door and put on his torch. Half raising the glass, he hesitated : better to wait and make it a convivial occasion.

The door opened suddenly : fortunately Reed was out of its way as it swung viciously, but he was not sufficiently clear to avoid the heavy body which strode through. As they cannoned, the Sergeant's glass slopped. Instinctively he looked down at the large puddle forming on one knee of a pair of dress trousers.

"What the hell are you doing, man?" said the voice of the D.C.

CHAPTER TWO

T HE OLD LADY had refused to go to bed. Perhaps
when you got to her age you needed no sleep at all,
thought the D.C. resentfully, irritated at the stain on his
left knee. It was the fourth time he had worn these
trousers. The Yard Control had had to send a car to a
very important place where the D.C. and his titled wife
were being vetted for the Governorship—Lady Sybil would
be joint *de facto* if not *de jure*—of a sunlit little Pacific
island now being groomed for the eventual control of her
institutions. Whitehall's policy of giving such tutelage by
means of the London police force might stand the D.C. in
good stead. The gathering had, he considered, reached that
urbane stage, just before the ladies went in search of their
rented mink, when the question was to be popped outright.
Instead the Big Man, slightly awed as amateurs were by
the dreary Scotland Yard piece, had pressed his hand and
whispered, "I am afraid a Squad Car has arrived for you,
my dear fellow. How you chaps do work!" That was that.
The way politicians forgot things he would have to do the
mole act all over again, perhaps for months, with all that
ground lost to rivals . . . There was a famous birching
headmaster from a private school in for it and a Brig. with
the world's record for presiding at courts martial. He
sighed and forced his thoughts back to the present and the
large uncomfortable Victorian dining-room. Quant's bald-
ing head was at the further end of the mahogany table,
about fourteen feet away, flanked by two inspectors and a
sergeant. Sally and Dick Cream, looking utterly weary,
were still being interviewed. For himself, the D.C. was

37

fighting a rearguard action with the Cream lawyer, a Mr Howe, a rangy man, tweedy at this hour even.

"I see no reason why you policemen should hang around upsetting the old lady," said Howe with the easy throw-it-away accent produced by better class English education.

"We have reason to believe a crime has been committed on these premises," countered the D.C.

In fact, immediately after being met at the door by Sergeant Jarvis, whose report was a model, he had thrown the twenty-odd plainclothes detectives from the seven squad vans into the job of searching the old house from roof to musty cellar. The cellar would be the place, thought the D.C. with smug triumph. Now this fellow—and he had to be taken gently because the American branch were legal advisers to the State Department—was trying to give them an ouster, lock, stock and barrel. Legally it was a dicey matter : a householder could order police off premises only to be faced quickly with a warrant to search. However, his brief specifically had 'no possible scandal' underlined. He closed his eyes briefly and saw the fronds of palm trees.

"I may have to order you off, old man," said Howe breezily.

"And let me come back with a search warrant and cause Mr Coroner to make Certain Observations?"

"Come off it!" They had certain clubs in common. "What the devil are your men clambering down into the cellar for? Giles got this spear in his back in a disused bedroom on the first floor."

"If you had wished to express an opinion, Mr Howe, you should have joined the police force say forty years ago in which case you might now be of sufficient rank to advise me of my business."

"Then I think you must go. And for the record my reason is fear for the health of dear old Mrs Cream. A lady of advanced years, in frail health."

The D.C., after seeing that Sergeant Reed was sent

38

home by car, had detailed Sergeant Jarvis to look after the old soul in her drawing-room.

"What the devil do you mean by incarcerating me with a walkin' medical encyclopaedia?" The door flew open and Mrs Cream glared in. The last dry kümmel he had had with the Big Man repeated itself as the D.C. glimpsed a bemused Sergeant Jarvis behind her.

With a carriage as trained as her voice (you could almost sense the boards being strapped on her spine) she balefully advanced. "He started with pains in the neck, and via wind round the heart, eventually reached the knee-caps."

It had been Waterloo for Jarvis. He had never met an old lady who could not be drawn into confidential conversation by the introduction of painful knee-caps.

"Since 1893," said Mrs Cream, "and God knows it was hard to get during two world wars, I have each morning quaffed the juice of a lemon in a pint of very hot water. I have never seen a doctor, apart from routine visits." She paused dramatically before advancing into the room and fixing the company with a scorching, outraged glance. The D.C. found himself struggling to establish the metric tonnage involved in hot water and lemon juice.

"What are policemen doing in my cellar? Don't lie to me. My ears are keen. I know every board in this old house."

"Madam," said the D.C. rising.

"Don't madam me. Where is that sensible policeman who drinks?"

"The trouble with grandmama," said Dick Cream in his rather light tenor, "is that she always wanted to do the heavy dramatic stuff. Irving thought she stank."

"At least he expressed himself with dignity." But she was laughing like a naughty girl. "But it is my house!"

The D.C. gave Quant a look. "Have you about finished up?"

"We have all the statements," said the Superintendent.
"Then ma'am," said the D.C. at his olde-worlde court-
liest, "may we repair to your small sitting-room? I am sure
I should be glad to join you in a small drink—"

He ushered the old lady ahead of him, whispering to
Jarvis that he might as well join the search parties. "And
tell them to be much quieter than they are."

Ambrose and Joan Cream—who currently shared an
apartment off Park Lane when in London—had been
dispatched home, rather protesting. Flitch, the American,
was staying at a surprisingly modest Bayswater hotel and
had been dropped off *en route*.

Mrs Cream clambered up on her commode. Sally and
Dick refused a drink, and, ignoring Quant (who did not
drink anyway) and the two inspectors (who assumed stiff
upper lips), the D.C. poured two pegs of whisky for himself
and the old lady, mentally quoting the regulation whereby
a police officer can drink on duty with the public for the
purposes of luring them or fooling them. He placed himself
on one of the sensible, elegant Windsor chairs.

"Mr Quant," he invited.

"It seems," said the Super, in the rather rich voice he
reserved for his addresses to the Women's Pleasant Hour at
his local chapel, "that the unfortunate gentleman passed
over at approximately 12.55. The doctor finds no reason to
contest this though it could have been earlier. Cause of
death was impalement through the back and into the vital
organs by means of a Roman style spear of the short kind.
Death took place within a couple of minutes and our doctor said that there would be no great pain, nothing in the
way of agony, so to speak."

"Are you saying he enjoyed it?" asked Sally, but unexpectedly subsided as her grandmother's eyes flicked over
her.

"I think we should have him laid out in my bedroom,"

declared Mrs Cream. "Perhaps you would send a car for my housekeeper, Rumming."

"I'm afraid that, 'um," said Quant, at a loss.

"Removed for autopsy." The old lady tried to drop her voice a full octave and succeeded in sounding like a parody of Margaret Rutherford. She was not with it, thought the D.C. Half of what he suspected might be a very wily old intelligence indeed was thinking of something else. Without appearing to do so he looked at Howe, the solicitor, seated next to Quant, elegant little notebook on one knee, slim gold pencil in one bony hand. The man was looking a little startled.

"It's best not to dwell on these things," soothed Quant.

"I always have been one for looking things in the face." The diction was impeccable as usual, but the old face had turned bleak. For once old Mrs Cream was not acting.

"Quite! Quite!" said the Super so that if the D.C. had not been staring at him he would have thought the fellow was rubbing his hands. "Quite! Now it seems that after dark this house is light-proof. There is an elaborate system of rubber roller blinds in excellent condition."

"Mr Blachford," said the old lady.

"Eh?"

"The odd job man. He comes once a fortnight. He repairs 'em."

They had not known that, thought the D.C. ruefully.

"Egress to the premises," rattled on Quant, abandoning his church voice for the official monotone, "can be obtained from the back, via in fact the street parallel to the main frontage. The family have long since used the back entrance for reasons of privacy. I may quote, though not verbatim, the words of the eldest grandchild: 'In our business privacy is often essential. Sometimes if we are trying something—a scene, an idea—space is necessary. Here we had both. Or it might be a business deal. There is a lot of mutual spying between the rival organisations. It suited us. Peter had the curtains put in—doing most of it himself—in about 1955.' "

"It was like coming on to a stage," said Sally, who was drooping forward away from the back of her chair. "Through the darkness of the old storeroom and then into blazing light. We were together and the world was outside."

Her words seemed to freeze off the bleakness of Quant's horse face. "Thus it seems," said the Super, "that in effect this ground floor is a self-contained flat, comprising the old dining-room, rarely used, a breakfast-room so-called which will in fact seat eight persons."

"Uncomfortable," said Mrs Cream.

"Be silent, darling," said Dick, "lest they put you in gyves."

"This small drawing-room," proceeded Quant, "Mrs Cream's bedroom, a bathroom and a small kitchen-cum-pantry. The three upstairs floors are unused except for two bedrooms kept up in case any of the family wish to stay. The room in which Mr Giles Cream met his death is a large old master bedroom, unfurnished except for various photographic-style lighting fixtures and miniature stages, toy affairs upon which various experiments were made. Apart from a patent air-conditioning device on this ground floor which pumps air in from outside, every window in the house is fast bolted. After six when the housekeeper, Mrs Rumming, and Mrs Cream's companion, Miss Birch, have left, the front door is kept locked."

There was an ugly little silence.

"None of us would have killed Giles," said Dick.

"So that leaves Mr Flitch or A. N. Other," said the D.C., feeling his voice hang tiredly in the air.

"Mr Flitch," said Quant, "would seem to be out of it. I do not think you heard Mr Ambrose Cream on the purpose of tonight's meeting, Commander, but, briefly, it was in connection with a very expensive forthcoming musical production. . . ."

The Commander had been with the senior inspector clambering around the thirty rooms of Larchmont before dismally looking at the huge damp cellar, divided for no apparent reason into two parts. Finally he had phoned for ten reinforcements, a matter of difficulty as skilled searchers were not much on duty at two in the morning. He had to enlist the aid of the two adjacent divisions to fill the quota.

Meantime Quant in the dining-room had been listening stolidly to Ambrose and Joan Cream. "We have a big deal on," said Ambrose, "the whole family that is. I do not wish to go into gory details. It is rumoured abroad, you can't keep things quiet today, but we like to keep the detailing sufficiently foggy about the edges. However, as usual we need money-men and to impress them finally we thought the kind of theatrical coup that echoes round the business would do no harm. We have been considering this for the past year, then it was Joan who discovered it. . . ."

Joan was a year older, recollected the Superintendent, forty as against thirty-nine, but she could have been five years younger as the harsh lighting beat down on her fair hair.

"Am—Ambrose—and I have the concert side of the business, Superintendent, and Sally, Giles and Dick the theatre. Sometimes, as in films, we coalesce and our interests are fluid. I was doing a coast to coast U.S. tour with a ballet company. By chance, the way things happen, I got snow-bound in a university. I thought, hell, I may as well be mildly cosy in there as hang around for flights which never appear. The only thing 'on' in the town was a recital by what turned out to be a Californian Mexican girl aged twenty-one. She had been on third-rate night club circuits, managed by a succession of no-goods and cheats. Somebody had conned her into giving a concert— God help us all—and inviting critics. Business-wise she does not know the time of day. It was all paper except my two dollars and similar from a booze artist salesman who thought it was strip. I have rarely heard such talent in the popular field. She is odd looking, but that is nothing, but with a magnificent figure and skin. Her voice runs along your spine : and she projects any emotion like some kind of searchlight. I'm being quite clinical. I went behind and signed her for three years. . . . Oh," she had caught Quant's eye, "if it goes well she'll become wealthy, the courts no longer enforce unfair contracts. Anyway at the moment and at our considerable expense she is having a pretty onerous series of courses in Italy. I thought it best to get her out of the U.S. And then . . ." she flicked a fore-finger at her brother.

"I was seated in my office one day when my assistant brought in Howard Flitch. He was originally English, now naturalised American. Ordinarily the conception and growth of a musical is a team effort. What Flitch tried was to write one holus-bolus in a cold-water apartment in Balti-more. He's got a sound background, conservatorium lec-turer etcetera, with a few one-performance compositions to his credit. The type that get one public presentation kind of thing. He couldn't get a hearing simply because nobody can do what he did. At that the lyrics were poor, it needed God knows what in the way of arrangement, cutting, tim-ing—oh, the lot. But we have a winner all right. We have got the two best lyric writers in the business, a dialogue man, a whole team. Fred Faust is incognito in Wales designing the sets. This time the year's greatest musical starts here and then goes *across* the Atlantic. Its title by the way is 'The Girl with the Roman Noise'."

44

"Beg your pardon, sir?" said the shorthand writer, "Did you say 'nose'?"

"*Noise*. The central character is Messalina : the theme is that imperialisms always have Messalinas. She travels back and forth in time."

"That would be the noise the Sergeant said he heard when he came in," said Quant, "coming off a tape recorder."

"If we broadcast our intent," said Cream, "there'd be a flood of cheapjack Messalina musicals rushed out. Well, at least one and I know the swine who'd do it. We cut some tapes of the various big numbers—there are performers who make a living by running through stuff—plus a lot of dialogue and patched it up on tape, as you would rough cut a film or roughly paste up illustrated printed matter. We were playing it over. Now, Giles and Sally—they were twins as you may know—have the two important non-singing parts. They have a song together, but they will mime it while a sound track is played. Would have, I should have . . ." Ambrose stopped, for a moment bogged down in the syntax troubles consequent upon homicide. "He must have gone upstairs to try that spear scene, although, damn it that's part of why we use this house, to try things out. There is an important scene where Messalina persuades her latest lover (the whole series of 'em were to be played by Giles) to pretend to take poison and throw himself back in a flower bed. Only the good lady has stuck a short spear among the blossoms. It was a scene Giles did not feel happy about visually. He was a rare fusser, we all of us are. He had the idea that if the slightest thing went wrong in the timing he'd just end up looking bloody ridiculous, suppressed titters and all that, the thing that makes actors wake up in a sweat."

"The spear came from where, sir?"

"I made it myself. There is a small but very well

equipped workshop attached to my office. I relax by making models, puttering with ideas for effects."

"It appears to have been fitted into a socket in a stand."

"Yes, the scene calls for a slave to fit the spear between the flowers and foliage as instructed by Messalina."

"Forgive me for harrowing your feelings, sir, but there was a cushion in front of the stand. Would it be true that Mr Cream would plump down backwards on the cushion with his back against the spearhead?"

"Yes. On stage there would be no cushion. Sally and Giles received about the best possible training," Ambrose paused for a fraction of a second while Quant stared at him, blandly. "And a certain amount of falling—it is only a knack—was part of it. I cannot understand it at all. The spear was essentially a thick rubber haft stained red with no bracing whatsoever and a head which I carved myself and painted with a black paint."

Quant had reached down and brought up a flat black box. Looking at it Sally had thought it one of the monster gift boxes of chocolates and felt her stomach turn.

"It has, er, been cleaned, sir," said Quant clumsily. Indeed, the police surgeon had scraped debris attached to the head into a small plastic box after the photographs had been taken and the fingerprint tests—negative—made. He took off the top. Sally stared at the floor.

"That isn't mine. May I?" asked Ambrose.

The Superintendent nodded and distastefully Ambrose took the three-foot weapon from the box, holding it between both hands.

"This isn't rubber."

"It is, so our technical man says, very flexible steel as a core to a rubber sleeve. Its flexibility might fool you at a casual touch. The head is a different matter. It is some kind of metal and razor sharp."

"It was . . ."

"Stuck in his back, right through the, er, great vessels.

46

He got up, wrenching it from the stand, staggered to the window and pressed the button which rolled the blind up. He probably didn't know much what was happening : our man says there would be no pain, merely discomfort."

"The colouring is different," grunted Ambrose, his wide-set blue eyes cold and squinting. "On stage you have to be careful with colour. I used a much lighter red than this : and my head was glossy paint, this is matt."

"Strange," said Quant, peering.

"Giles was colour-blind, as colour-blind as you can get, and please will you put that thing away before I'm sick," said Joan.

They watched the Superintendent replace the spear and close the lid.

"Now, would you know who benefits by his death?"

"Benefits? Oh, yes, it is obviously murder I suppose. I read somewhere that gain is never a motive for a wealthy person, and we are wealthy." Ambrose sounded very weary. "Giles had two ex-wives, both settled up handsomely and fully paid off. He had three children, all with settlements in trust, aged fourteen, nine and seven. What he leaves will eventually go to the children."

"And what will he leave?"

Ambrose shrugged. "He was one of the top, say fifteen, actors in this country; take your pick as to his actual rating. He turned away work. I suppose his immediate assets would be somewhere around fifteen thousand : his only real estate was a small country cottage. There is an expensive car. He had a fifth interest in the family business, nominally capitalised at sixty thousand pounds. What it is worth as of now will take months of haggling with Somerset House. The company owns theatre leases and substantial holdings. Say his value for duty might be two hundred and fifty thousand pounds. I do not know what assurance he carried. I always advised him to keep it pretty heavy for tax purposes."

"You'd be the business brains of the family, sir?"

"To a point. I forced myself to take a qualification, enough to know what the figure-men are talking about. But you can take it from me that Giles was not murdered for his money."

"Then what was it?"

"I'm honestly damned if I know," Ambrose had said slowly.

Listening to the unemotional recital of this scene in Mrs Cream's drawing-room, the Deputy Commander with half his mind was praying that the door would open and a triumphant inspector enter with the tidings that the Dockern Hoard had been discovered. By God, he'd put the whole lot of them in the nick overnight, thought the D.C., except for the American fellow and the old lady. Better get a matron and a nurse in for her, thought the D.C., to cut off any waffle about police brutality. Yet nothing happened. The Superintendent's voice stopped, and there was a yawning quality about the air. The D.C. had to do something fast.

"Mrs Cream," he said, looking up at the old lady who seemed the only one of them untired, except for the solicitor, Howe, "I think in the circumstances we should leave you adequately guarded, with a matron to boot."

"It is a long time since I kicked anything," said Mrs Cream. "In fact not since I played a petulant debutante in the summer of 1903—the play ran for four days, I remember. I suppose you mean a police matron?"

"I really meant a kind of nurse."

"Mental, I suppose!"

"You are determined to have me on the wrong foot."

48

"Have you something peculiar in your mind about feet, harping about them as you do, young man?"

Of course, she was just about old enough to have listened to Oscar and his friends in the flesh at the Café Royal, thought the D.C. mournfully, but Mrs Cream abruptly softened.

"I do not require nursing services, but the comfort of sturdy policemen—if they take their boots off in the house—would be a joy. I much suspect that there is a homicidal maniac roaming the streets."

With an inward triumph the D.C. saw a ripple of annoyance over the lawyer's face. With luck he could persuade the old lady to keep police in her house for some days, and no ingenious device of the human mind could withstand skilled searchers for more than twenty-four hours. Come to think of it, there might be something fishy around that ruddy backyard. The Victorians went in for concealed coal bunkers and stuff like that. And for himself, and probably Quant, it was time for bed. He had half risen, feeling the creaks in his knees and numbness in his hams when there was a sharp tattoo of knocks on the door leading to the storeroom. A plump but agile inspector, until now seated mouselike near it, moved like a swiftly bouncing ball, pushing the door outward, but rebounding from its surface.

"Now, now," said a cold clear voice, "mind what you are doing there! Do you want to knock my good tooth out?"

The door opened and a very tall man with wavy, iron-grey hair surmounting a very fair-skinner, long but regular-featured face, stood there gently smiling.

"I was passing the front," he said amiably, "and there was light blazing forth. I told my chauffeur to turn and park in the other road." He paused as if that was enough.

"Commander," said Ambrose, getting to his feet, "this is Herr Sven-Eric Grädde, a Swedish friend."

49

"We know each other," said the visitor, extending his hand.

A good memory, thought the D.C. as he returned the greetings. It was fully three years since he had met the Swede at a reception given by an industrialist who somehow felt safer if there were a few socially well-connected policemen around him. Sven-Eric himself was a multi-millionaire, he believed, the head of a minor—as they went—industrial empire which, however, he owned personally.

"A dreadful thing has happened," said Dick decisively, "my brother Giles is dead, perhaps murdered. It happened here tonight."

Sven-Eric's jaw dropped momentarily, and he made a small abrupt bow to old Mrs Cream, sitting motionless.

"There is nothing for me to say," he said softly, "except an apology for this intrusion." He turned on his heel.

"I'm sorry, Herr Grädde," said the D.C., "but sooner or later you will have to make a statement concerning your presence here tonight."

"I will do it now if that is convenient. I understand police procedure. You know my name and who I am. I have been in this country for two months. With certain associates I am interested in a business project, as yet in embryo form, with the Cream interest. My discussions have been held here, for reasons of security. It is an affair with tricky ramifications, you understand. Now I am a man who cannot sleep at night without recourse to drugs, of which I disapprove"—he was a big, fit looking fellow, thought the D.C. enviously—"I can only sleep during the day, and then only among the noises of a city. So for years my rule has been to sleep from 7 until 12 a.m." He shrugged. "It has its advantages, but I'll spare you the clinical details. Tonight I had no business to think of : my head ached, so my chauffeur drove me, which I find soothing." He paused, head bent.

50

The D.C. noticed that he wore a magnificent Italian blue silk suit. He was remembering Sven-Erik more clearly. Not untypical in some ways of one type of his countrymen: coldish voice oddly superimposed upon a slightly ingratiating manner, the feeling that inside might be all kinds of tension.

"On impulse I directed the driver here hoping I might find the younger Creams in conclave," the Swede continued. "Sometimes they worked here most of the night. I intended having the chauffeur park a few hundred yards away where Giles, Dick and Ambrose used to park their cars: it is a discreet cul-de-sac. If the cars were there, I thought I'd drop in, at any rate for a drink. Then I saw the lights blazing and wondered . . ."

"That will be all, sir," said the D.C. smoothly. "If we should want a signed statement, for the record as you understand no doubt, I will be in touch. Inspector, pray escort Mr Grädde to his car."

He waited until the door of the storeroom closed and turned to the others.

"Mrs Cream, I will see that the men I leave on guard do not disturb you. Would any of you require a lift home in a police car?"

They shook their heads.

"Then the Superintendent and I will bid you good-night."

In the hallway they met the inspector in charge of the search operations. He slightly shook his head and pointed one thumb downwards. In a low voice the D.C. said: "Keep four men patrolling the outside of the house. There is the barest chance we might have a maniac around. Is the roof clear?"

"Yes, sir, nobody up there. We'll have to wait until dawn to look for hidey-holes."

"Keep your men out of sight and for God's sake noise-less, and continue the inside operation. A housekeeper comes in at eight and a companion at nine. Arrange a change of shifts, including yourself, at ten. I leave the briefings to you. Perhaps you should get Inspector Prinsep."

"Yes, sir," the Inspector bridled slightly with pleasure.

"I don't mind staying on, Commander," said Quant as they went out the door.

"I'll see you in my office at 1.15." The Commander cut him short. "We both need six hours sleep. Check that you have a car sent to collect you. Use your electric razor on the journey and have ten minutes more sleep."

The Superintendent who scraped away with one of a nest of cut-throat razors wished him goodnight.

CHAPTER THREE

At five to one next afternoon the D.C., smelling of strong bath salts, found Quant already seated sanctimoniously in the waiting-room, a thick file on one bony knee. Probably been in an hour or more, thought the D.C. without emotion.

"Sleep well?"

"Yes, Commander."

It was a mystery to the D.C. how Quant's proverbial state of flatulence never interfered with his slumbers. The sleep of the just was impervious to nervous dyspepsia he supposed. "Come in," he invited.

"Well, I suppose you have the news, Commander," said Quant.

Bad news, of course, thought the D.C., not answering as he glanced at the few papers in his 'in' basket. A slip of paper conveyed the hierarchical order that for the next forty-eight hours all his energies must be devoted to the death of Giles Cream. His pending work had neatly disappeared into the well-oiled machine (actually to the desk of another Deputy Commander who was currently nearing apoplexy).

"Mm? I haven't seen anything interesting except a hurriedly consumed kipper."

"Inspector Prinsep came on the line at twelve-thirty, sir. He begs to report that there is no sign of any secret cavity, receptacle or other means of concealment in the dwelling-place known as Larchmont," said the Super, the file open before him. "That includes the cellar, the roof, and the yard behind the house, plus the bit of front garden and the superficial drains."

There were searchers, inspired searchers and Inspector Prinsep. False cappings upon teeth, car fittings of solid gold underneath the paint, cavities concealed under heavy baths, bidets with hollow sides, brickwork actually cemented over the front of safes—all these were the merest routine to him before he put his narrow, search-light intellect to more ingenious speculations. A teddy bear carried by a toddler did not bring a paternal smile to Prinsep, merely the thought of the amount of heroin the inside could conceivably contain. He had successfully removed bandages from chronic sufferers and once discovered stolen jewels in a bombe alaska. Unconsciously, the D.C. screwed his mouth into a small 'o' as if he had sucked a lemon.

"I told them to start all over again." Quant did not sound enthusiastic.

"About this fellow Reed," said the D.C. "I think he has gone far enough, reeling about on the job half slopped and slopping. In view of his past services, he can take the easy way with a pension *pro rata* and I'll sign the reference myself. I understand he does not need money, for reasons never satisfactorily explained to me. If he cares to take it the hard way, we'll appoint a superintendent to report officially."

Quant cleared his throat, a longish process. The D.C. sat and stared.

"You may have noticed that Reed is a very lucky man," said the Super. "He should be a Chief Inspector by now and I'll admit that my signature has been and will be one of the obstacles in his way to further promotion. But to give him his due he has recovered—I was looking at the figures on the check list the other day—more stolen property in terms of value than any other man we have. He has the knack of blundering upon the soft corn of the criminal."

The D.C. was basically a fair man. "It cannot be luck," he said. "I admit his record, but deplore his drunkenness, the unsavouriness of his reputation and the odour of violence which his cases often attract. And what about his impression on the public!"

"The English are boozers at heart." Quant gave a melancholy head shake. "The Pastor and I have to wrestle with this tendency constantly—in others, of course," he hastened to add. "The complaints about Reed—the man he was alleged to have thrashed in a cellar, for one—come from the beastliest kind of criminal. As for last night, old Mrs Cream liked him, as she said, and the two youngest Creams mentioned that he had handled the original situation with great tact. I might suggest, sir, that we give him a roving brief on this case. He has the nose, as you say, and, I still maintain, the luck. And if you will excuse me, I feel in my bones . . ."

"And in mine, Mr Quant. I fear we are postponing an evil hour, but you are probably right. Where is the feller? Snoring like a hog I'll be bound."

"He has amazing powers of recuperation. He was in around ten, or so I was told when I arrived, and is assisting the compilation of the running report."

"Get him down," said the D.C. "There is nothing we can do until the complete laboratory reports come through, and that'll be an hour yet."

The Superintendent pushed over the file and took up the intercom. "Quant here, good morning to *you*. Perhaps you will join me in the Commander's office in ten minutes."

The D.C., as were most of his colleagues, was a fast reader and knew many of the facts already. He had flipped rapidly through the ten quarto sheets of double spacing that comprised the file by the time a knock at the door heralded Sergeant Reed.

Damn the man, thought the D.C. Drunks should be bleary, unshaven, bootlaces not done up, socks slopping down, hand uncontrollable in their tremulous activity, hair unkempt. Reed was immaculately groomed from his white

55

shirt and chaste tie, forty guinea grey suit, down to his polished red leather shoes which the D.C. recognised as coming from the bespoke trade. Only his darkish glasses were a drunk's slight betrayal.

"Good morning, gentlemen," he said, in his usual lightish, pleasant voice devoid of accent and, when you listened carefully, without much expression.

"Sit down," said the D.C. If the fellow was nervous he showed no sign. "Three coffees," he spoke down the intercom. "Now Mr Reed we want your thoughts. As you will know from the reports, we are up the proverbial gum-tree."

He wondered what happened up gum-trees except koala bears.

"I have only a couple of points, sir," said the Sergeant, hands in lap. "A minor one I dare say is why Herr Grädde should carry a torch with him. He must have had one. Nobody could get in that back way without one, even though it was not a terribly dark night. He said he ordered his chauffeur out there on impulse. He might have carried one in the car, I suppose it is one of those elaborate affairs with things built in, or the chauffeur might have provided it. I think it should be checked."

"Herr Grädde is international capitalism personified," said the D.C. "The Creams want him, not the other way about."

"Nevertheless, I've made a note of it." Reed's cool assumption that he would continue on the case did not pass unnoticed or unresented. "The second point is that at the time there was a scuttlebut around that Peter Cream, who died while testing a car, might have been helped along."

"You mean murdered?" The D.C. sat bolt upright.

Reed shrugged. "I suppose it came to that. I dug the old file out half an hour ago. He was aged thirty-five and a consultant to various automobile companies. Reputedly he had turned down half a dozen offers of top-of-the-ladder jobs. The firm he owned held some lucrative patents and his ambition centred round this area. Anyway he was testing a sports car prototype which was unsatisfactory. The fee if he provided a cure was to be a record one. He wasn't a famous racing driver, although for experience he had driven a couple of seasons as number four in a works team. Competent was the word used about him. Anyway one morning at eleven he was ambling round the track at not more than an estimated 80 m.p.h.—there were experienced observers. He went into a sharpish S bend and did not straighten out. The car rolled broadside on after it hit the sandbags. Then it caught fire. Nothing strange about that, because it was a prototype and not meant to be turned over. It was just after I became a sergeant and it was Superintendent Hildebrand's last case before retirement. The file had the annotation : 'Sergeant Reed reported to me that he had heard certain rumours to the effect that the car had been tampered with. There is no evidence upon this point suitable to be placed before the Coroner.' I may say that I have not the slightest recollection of making this report, though I can find out on which jobs I was working at the time. I was not attached to the Cream accident at all. The body was charred beyond recognition, and the Ministry Inspector could make nothing out of the partly fused burned-out car. Verdict was 'Death by Misadventure'. A doctor gave evidence that Peter Cream had a medium-serious case of hypertension and that his blood pressure tended to creep up. He was on pills and a low-salt-content diet which he tended to forget. A *bon viveu*r as far as food was concerned, a homosexual with the usual tensions, and reputedly a pot smoker. Do you think I should look into it? Two sudden deaths in a family sometimes means double murder."

The D.C. said, "I do wish, Sergeant, you would realise

that Mr Quant and I are two grannies to whom teaching is repugnant. No, no, we all had a lousy night indeed," said the D.C. magnanimously. "By all means dig a little. The ten-year gap is the negative indication, though there have been cases . . . but I mustn't teach you to suck eggs. Anything else?"

Reed hesitated, then shook his head.

"I think you had better listen to this," said Quant, using the Sergeant as a stalking horse. "The time factors are worrying. We might start at 5.30, at which time Giles Cream got into his Chelsea flat. His manservant deposes that he had a shower and then changed into the dark suit in which he died. As was his frequent habit he had what forty years ago would have been known as a high tea, centred around smoked fish and poached egg, a dish of which he was fond. Giles watched his eating habits, and he very often had this kind of meal around six and nothing further until he took a few biscuits and a glass of sherry before going to bed, generally about one in the morning when he was working. He finished eating at approximately 6.45. His man lives in and at seven, when he had put the dirty dishes into the sink, Giles rang for him and said he would not want anything more for that day. So it was round to the pub for a drink, supper and a game of darts. When the man returned at ten the flat was empty. Giles's bedroom door was open and the man looked in. He then went to his own quarters—room plus bathroom—watched the TV until eleven and went to bed. Since his last divorce three years ago Giles's mistress has been one Mrs Hedi Ching. We've all heard of her. No legalisation of the situation was intended it seems," said Quant disapprovingly (half of the Free Church membership of north London had lost their income tax privilege as single persons as the result of Quant's nagging).

"Howsoever," said the Superintendent, "it being a good hour from the flat to his grannie's, it must have been after eight, say nearer eight-thirty that he reached Larchmont. Of the others, the schedule is : Sally Cream, who drove up from her house near Reading, arrived at Larchmont at ten; Dick Cream at quarter past ten; and Joan and Ambrose, together, at something after eleven. All that is the grist we have to mill today.

"The serious matter is that there is no independent authority for Giles's arrival or movements at Larchmont. We may get more from the two brothers and the two sisters when we go over the preliminary statements today." The Superintendent licked his lips.

Doodling on his scratch pad, the D.C. wondered if the unfortunate Creams realised what the next forty-eight hours held for them. The veiled threats punctuated by crude cajolery were not for the gentry; instead would be the endless harping upon the original form of the statement : "This does not appear to be quite clear, madam, perhaps we could go over it again."

"By independent," said Reed slowly, "you must mean the old woman."

"Exactly, Mr Reed. Joan and Ambrose had brought a hamper which apparently was the custom. On the occasion of these family gatherings there was a kind of buffet spread out in the breakfast room. If you were hungry you wandered in and helped yourself to one of the delicacies packed by Fortnum and Mason. Giles who was, I will not use the term food faddist, the odd man out as far as eating habits were concerned, rarely touched it apart from a dry biscuit or so."

"Drink?" said the D.C.

"This is the very first roundup," warned Quant, "but there is no evidence so far that he imbibed to excess. Working actors rarely do, so Records tell me. The ones who do do not work if you follow me." He could not resist cocking a pair of cold grey eyes in the direction of Sergeant Reed. "His brothers and sisters merely say that Giles

59

was there; Ambrose says he spoke of his dissatisfaction with the business with the spear. The apparatus, together with a lot of other stuff, was kept on the top floor of the old house which has been used as a combination junk and property room. We have not yet itemised it all. Now old Mrs Cream, talking to Sergeant Jarvis, does not seem at all clear when, or even if, Giles appeared on the scene."

"A clever old lady," said the D.C. "When they are old *and* clever it's hell."

"The medical evidence," said Quant, "is that deceased could well have died at 12.55 p.m. It is not conclusive. Examination of the cadaver was at 1.35 p.m. Given certain conditions of heating death could have occurred as early as 9 p.m., although not much earlier; you understand what I am getting at, Sergeant?"

"I did not mention it," said Reed, "for fear of confusing the issue unnecessarily, but I could not swear that the man who looked out that window was anybody in particular except somebody with blond hair, dressed in a man's clothes. I only saw Giles on stage or in newspaper and magazine photographs. It could have been any of the Creams except the old lady, who is rounder in the face and not very like them. I don't know about Jarvis, but I'd make a very bad witness."

Some of these Pacific Islands, ruminated the D.C., had marvellous ways of cooking pig. In her declining years, as he considered them, Lady Cynthia had grown very partial to pork and long autobiographies. A lieutenant-governorship had never seemed more desirable. He forced himself to speak mildly.

"I think that what you are working round to, Superintendent, is that Mr Reed, in his inimitable fashion should be asked to worm his way into Mrs Cream's confidence," said the D.C. "A good idea I think. Spare no expense, Sergeant. These old ladies develop likes and dislikes. An old auntie I once had liked the cheapest kind of toffee, the stuff you buy in slab form and crack with a hammer. She left sixty thousand pounds to my cousin who used to take her a pound of it when he called. Sometimes it's conversation. Bone up on the plays running in the early nineteen twenties with plenty of names! Oh, well, here I am trying to teach you! And there is her cook-housekeeper, Mrs Rumming. That class of person always like drink. Get her in the private bar with a couple of port and lemons, that sort of thing."

"Their drinking habits have changed," said Reed, unable to let a bibulous solecism pass unchecked.

"Babychams, then," said the D.C. "And the other old bitch, Miss Birch, the companion, probably goes in for weak tea with a slug of something in it on the sly. Carry a flask with you and ply her with it!"

"I must say," said Sergeant Reed, "that with due respect I don't like the hidden treasure bit. It's based, as far as the file has it, on far too many suppositions. Kids of that age knowing values! Mostly in the pre-teen group it's just tinsel and food values which attract 'em. Ask any probation officer what they pinch, and it isn't motivated by hard cash."

"Peter, the eldest, was fourteen," said the D.C. "As far as I can work it out he was *clever* and talented. The siblings are talented. There is a difference as you know."

"The old lady might be a hard case," persisted Reed.

"Old people," said the D.C., thinking of almost forgotten and deceased relatives, "hate as well as any of us, but the point is that they rarely have the energy to do anything about it."

"Can I have Sergeant Jarvis along?" asked Reed resignedly. "We complement each other."

"Very well," said the D.C. "You will work together. One final word. I just might be wrong about the existence of treasure, but this case seems to me to have an odour of money around it."

61

Reed nodded and went in search of Jarvis whom he found seated on one of the benches in the corridor to the canteen looking up the regulations. He was in fact four pounds and eightpence in front as the result of his night's work, but at this stage in the game he felt the usual urge to raise it until the next pound. If you moved dead bodies you could be—under the Special Emoluments Minute of 1923—entitled to the sum of fourteen shillings, enabling you in those pre-welfare State days to have a medical check-up. Yet the Minute specifically excluded death by accident, gunshot wounds or the results of an affray. On the whole, the Sergeant was of the opinion that he might chance his arm. The remaining six and fourpence could be put down to dry cleaning, which was almost impossible to disprove. He would have liked to ask Reed, but the man was notoriously cavalier about expenses.

"It appears to be large chunks of money," said Reed and aroused a flicker of interest. He summarised the report.

"If Prinsep can't find it it's not there," said Jarvis gloomily putting his expense sheet in his wallet. "I'll take cook and the companion, eh, and you see the old lady?"

Reed drove his own car. "What did you make of 'em last night?"

"I find actors difficult," said Jarvis. "I wouldn't say that the Creams had much life apart from their work. That sort of people! I just don't think murder would enter their minds except as a stage effect."

"I might be able to pick up some gossip about Giles," said Reed, "though the newspaper tittle-tattle about him was always pretty innocuous. Two undefended divorces, 'adultery with an unknown woman', no suggestion of hard feelings."

There were three police cars outside Larchmont, two newspaper reporters and a photographer.

"Anything for us, Sarge?"

"You know near as much as I do. Giles Cream was

found stabbed. There doesn't seem any reason why he should have been."

One of the reporters gave him a rather sly look.

The door was opened by a spare woman in her sixties. When you looked at her, you saw that she was beautiful in a dark, memorable way quite different from the bright, bold beauty of the Creams.

"Would you be Miss Birch?" asked Jarvis.

She nodded.

"Perhaps we could have a little talk," said Jarvis, "somewhere where I can give my poor feet a rest, if you'll excuse me. I'm Sergeant Jarvis. This is Sergeant Reed who has called to see Mrs Cream."

"We'll go into the sitting-room, Mr Jarvis," said Miss Birch. "Mr Reed will find Mrs Cream in the breakfast room enjoying her, um, coffee."

The old lady was seated where she could see out of the window to the front gate. She had finished a pear and was pouring rum into her coffee, and looked up as Reed went in.

"Ah, you are the agreeable policeman who takes a sociable glass. Please pour for yourself. It is a very old bottle, but in the circumstances . . ."

She stared absent-mindedly at the portraits upon the mantelpiece "When it does not matter, you don't *want* to eat much. As a girl I could not carry weight well, and my life seemed an agony of hunger."

"You've been in this house a fair number of years, ma'am."

"I took it after my son was born. I bought the expiry of the lease and an annuity. It seemed the best way : I come of a long lived family. My son and daughter-in-law fell over a cliff. They were a happy-go-lucky pair. . . . Well, I was left with the children. I had been fortunate that it is a biggish house. Every year the money seems to shrink. I took a job, reading play-scripts, something I could do here.

I was never much of an actress, but in those days I knew what people liked and whether the play could be staged. Everybody was writing plays then." She shrugged frail shoulders.

"Did you know the Dockerns?"

"I first knew the uncle of Lord Dockern. Rather unusually I got to know the family. The late Lord was a boy and I suppose he had a juvenile crush on me. Anyway I sent him a wedding present and regular Christmas cards. I met his wife a couple of times. When war came, I was naturally worried, remembering the zeppelins, so when the evacuation scheme was announced I telephoned Lady Dockern, suggesting that as they would have children parked on them, they might choose the devils they knew something of. They were quite agreeable. Dockern got them into schools. I had a war-job, but I saw them five or six times. It seemed so safe. Then it happened. I may say that the eldest boy, Peter, was remarkably capable, far beyond his years. No doubt it was partly due to him that they survived. They came back—I met them at the station, each carrying their own suitcase. Ah! I gave up the job and looked after them. We slept under the stairs in three of those little metal shelters. The children never talked about their experience, but they were very normal. I don't think it did anything to them, except maybe Peter. He became extremely precocious."

"It must have cost a fortune to educate them. I understand they all had higher education."

"They worked their way through college," she said proudly. "Oh, Peter was the mainspring of it all. He took it all off my shoulders. And it seemed in no time they were all making money."

Hm, thought Reed. She might have believed it. Peter sounded a very plausible type. He finished the rum and thanked her. "Should you think of anything . . ." he said in parting.

"I have racked my brains," she said. "I can think of nothing."

He found Jarvis looking rather dazed. Miss Birch had for years collected illustrated chocolate boxes under the impression they were valuable. By Mrs Cream's permission her choicest items were stored in the house and some of these she was displaying, opining meantime that whoever had stabbed poor Mr Giles might well have been after them.

Jarvis caught Reed's eye and shook his head. They left her carefully repacking the boxes in two mammoth old suitcases.

"Knows nothing," whispered Jarvis. "Does the shopping and waits on the mistress, but the only things in her head are chocolate boxes."

The cook, Mrs Emily Rumming, was in the kitchen and amid a fine aroma of sherry. She saw Reed looking at the bottle. "It's my pore nerves," she announced, "Mr Giles was like me own sons. More, 'cause they bin in quad for three years and got another six to go. You musta 'eard of the Rumming boys, 'aven't you?"

"Yes, indeed," said Reed.

"Afraid of nothing they're not. 'Ere, 'ave a glarst of the fruity. The Missus give it to me when she saw 'ow I trembled."

Reed swiftly poured himself a generous slug. Mrs Cream was no fool. It came from Cyprus.

"Any idea who did it, ma'am?"

"He wouldn't have an enemy in the world," she said. "He was eighteen when I came here twenty years ago. Cheese soufflés," she said mysteriously and gave a gusty sigh. "The fambly give me tickets to most of the hits, and I've watched him his first bit parts upwards. Nobody would want to 'urt him."

Jarvis's brand of unction, and his skilled introduction of painful ailments (most of which Mrs Rumming had had)

65

unlocked veritable floodgates, but it was apparent that the good lady knew nothing much. The family were not around often during the day, and her acquaintance with them was mostly a matter of Christmas gifts and free tickets.

On their way out they met Inspector Prinsep, a squat, rather worried man. He threw his hands up. "Nothing here," he said. "Will you tell Mr Quant? I'm wanted over at Finchley. Emphasise nothing at all."

It was four o'clock. Even as he registered the fact of 'tea money' Jarvis sighed and looked at Reed. "No point in going back to the madhouse," said his senior. "Ever heard of a Mrs Hedi Ching? She was Giles's mistress."

Jarvis nodded sardonically. Few people had not heard of Mrs Ching, since her first marriage and divorce at the age of sixteen. She had been a near champion swimmer at the time. Another three husbands later, Mrs Ching's press cuttings must fill a lengthy shelf. She had the peculiar knack of either being with important people or visiting places when things were happening. Sometimes she got into gaol—once in China, once in Louisiana—but officialdom always let her out. A few of her friends were notorious, but scandal of the type which was frowned upon by her contemporaries had never tarred her. She lived, when in London, in a tiny, elegant Queen Anne box, doing her entertaining, however, at her Sussex estate.

"You going to see her?" asked Jarvis.

"Might as well."

It would mean tea money, thought Jarvis as they drove, and this hour Mrs Ching could hardly fail to cough up a coffee and biscuits.

A maid showed them into the first floor's tiny salon. Something over thirty, the lady was no less attractive for having muscles. Her silver blond hair was set off by perfect skin, slightly tanned. There were tell-tale marks of tears as she looked at them out of big grey eyes.

66

"Perhaps you will have coffee?"

There might be cakes, thought Jarvis as he agreed. They were in fact tiny almond tarts. Reed sighed gently and took only coffee.

"It is about Giles, of course," she said. "His grandmother was kind enough to ring me this morning. I never met her."

Old Mrs Cream had a certain fellow feeling, thought the Sergeant, an old bird but once of similar feather. As though she read his thoughts, Mrs Ching said, "Giles Cream and I had been having a big *affaire* for two years."

"Were you planning on marrying?"

"We both rather felt a little tired of the altar bit," she said in her husky voice. "And it would have seriously affected our income tax position."

"Did you know much about his financial position, where the money came from?"

"Good heavens, he was one of the top actors! He turned down the earth, but the earth, to make a film in Italy only a week before his death."

"I don't mean income. I mean capital," said Reed. "He seemed to be able to raise large sums."

She was nobody's fool. The eyes momentarily narrowed, but she said slowly, "I did think he had some inherited money or perhaps that the family as a whole did."

Reed shrugged, and watched Jarvis skilfully pick up two biscuits at once. "It's just that we like to build up a complete picture. What was he like?"

She showed emotion for the first time. "Oh, he was a serious man, well-read and thoughtful. He could be witty, but not cruelly so at all, not ever. What got under his skin was injustice. He was extremely sensitive about that. And he adored his grandmother. They used to make jokes about her, but down deep she was a martinet. Nobody offended Grannie. Oh, Giles was ambitious. I gathered they are an ambitious family—I don't know the others very well—and

67

that Giles might have been the least so. There is a hard streak in them, particularly Ambrose."

"And you do not know who killed him?"

She hesitated a little. "People don't shoot actors, do they? You remember what Maugham said about actors' hearts. I express myself clumsily, but I do not think that Giles's passions went deep enough to murder or attract murder. Except perhaps where his grandmother was involved or gross injustice. When you can simulate any emotion, as Giles could, pretence and actuality have no boundary."

"You mean they are phonies?" said Jarvis, wiping crumbs off his chin on to the pale rose carpet.

"Good actors can't be phonies."

"I'm afraid we are just two middle-rank policemen Mrs Ching, and what you've been saying spells out phoney for me."

"Oh, he was not. I told you that injustice aroused him." She stopped. "This is part of the international technique is it not? Make people good and mad to see what they will say. Well, gentlemen, I have told you all I know."

"And very helpful you have been," said Reed as he opened the door.

"I have a pricking in my thumbs," said Reed, getting into the car.

"Me, too, the fellow was up to something. Where does she get her money?"

"First husband was an oil billionaire, the third a South American mining tycoon. I presume from settlements."

"Half a mo'," said Jarvis. "Look at that."

That was a taxi drawn up outside Mrs Ching's house and a tall dark, ugly man was paying the driver.

"That's Flitch, the musician who was with the Creams."

Reed took his word for it, his memories of the night's proceedings being foggy at the edges.

"This should be reported." He looked at his watch. "Tell you what, Jarvis, I'll drop you back and you see

Quant. I'll park the car and use a taxi." He saw Jarvis's face fall at the thought of losing an opportunity so fraught with expense money. "Oh, the Super will have some dirty but comfortable job for you nobody else wants to touch. Perhaps Flitch, but don't forget Americans are entitled to complain to their embassy."

"Ah," said Jarvis reflectively and licked his lips.

Reed presently found a cab and, from his extensive knowledge, chose a curious pub, off the theatre district, which catered for the entertainment industry at various levels. In a large but fusty (its windows were immovable) 'Snuggery' customarily sat of an evening certain razor-scarred 'doormen' from the strip joints, fortifying themselves for the night's work, while feminine company was provided by the usual presence of four or five notorious young procuresses. The smart 'Lounge' served as a convenient meeting place for the managers of the casinos; the 'Public' had its congregation of betting shop owners and boxing promoters. But it was the 'Lounge Bar' in which Reed was interested. It was a long, narrow room with three entrances to the street, horribly draughty for this reason, but with an illusion of warmth by reason of its preposterous but genuine Victorian decor, nowadays worth a small fortune. Red plush and Dutch metal were the predominant impression; little stalls, like confessional boxes open at the back, jutted out periodically from the bar with its golden railings smelling of Brasso. People could walk through, sly-glancing at the company, choosing somebody they might want to meet. Jobs that were 'going' could be traded as on a stock exchange, a fiver perhaps borrowed from somebody who had landed a lucrative 'shop'. Perhaps it was only half a pint of bitter and a slice of the heavy ham-and-egg pie that you hoped would be forthcoming. It was a place of unreality and illusion inhabited by illusionists. The managers and agents were much too fly to venture in.

69

Reed settled for Old Beggs, the juggler, looking like a second-hand dealer in his aged blue serge suit that stank, when you got close up, of sweat, beer, vinegar and fish oil, these things mainly comprising Begg's life. A fine juggler, who now no longer had to think of the extraordinary things his thick hands did. Beggs had travelled the world and seen little of it but stale dressing-rooms, the square of board he performed upon, and bars. "Ar," he said to Reed, "don't see you around much." Then with the ego-centricity typical of his life he told the Sergeant he was leaving the following night for a tour of South Africa, Singapore, Australia and New Zealand. "Only way to make yer dough these days, and it's away from the family, thank Gawd. Bring 'em up, grammar school and all, and put 'em steady in banks and wot happens? Them and the stuck up birds they marry get ashamed of you."

Although he rarely appeared to listen, by some process all current theatrical gossip was to be found in Beggs's head, possibly because he spent his days around licensed premises and absorbed it impartially and without much interest, like a turned-on tape-recorder.

"I'm interested in the Creams."

"One of them died last night," said Beggs without emo-tion. "Stabbed somebody was saying. Giles it was, the young 'un."

"You knew him?"

"Years ago when he was in rep he used to come in. A lot of them drop out of this," Beggs jerked his thumb, "after a few months. 'Young Moneyman', he was called. Flashing it about, and plenty of people here to hold out a hand, talking of forming his own company. Probably some inheritance was what he was throwing down the sink. Somebody might have taken him aside for the Dutch uncle business or else the lolly ran out, because he stopped com-ing here or the other places. Have one with me."

Reed chose a double Scotch.

"Who'd know him?"

Beggs squinted round his raddled nose and stepped back a few paces.

"Old Alfred down there might be a bet. He toured South America with Giles last year. Scenes from the Bard, cultural stuff." Beggs looked as though he could spit. "Giles always used to give him a small part when he was Barding. Tell you what, he's been out for nine months, on the Old Age. I fancy a steak myself, so suppose we buy him one. Set him up! Oh, Lord, not here. There's a place along the road."

Alfred might have been seventy or more. A tall man, slightly stooped, with flashing black eyes and a well fitting toupée. He recoiled slightly until Beggs said the invitation was on account of his imminent South African trip.

"Keep out of politics, old man," said Alfred as they ate a first course of crayfish. "They pop you in the gaol there."

"One thing in our trade," said Beggs, after a swig of hock, "we keep out of politics. I don't know anything about these bloody countries except the going price of grog and don't bloody well want to."

"I'd have agreed with you entirely, but I've met a few, comics and character actors doing light comedy, who were militant Tories." He mentioned a few names. "You rarely meet a lead who is political—too engrossed in the stage. But there, and it isn't maligning him, there was young Giles Cream, God rest him."

"Political?" asked Reed.

"Always a touch on the romantic side, Anthony Hope sort of stuff. Intrigue in high places. Remains of childhood daydreams, I imagine. He had a nasty time in the war, was probably accustomed to fantasy as a crutch. I really struck it when I toured South America with him last year. He had . . ." he hesitated.

"Mrs Hedi Ching with him?" asked Reed.

"Yes, I sometimes forget everybody knows. She seemed

71

to know every goddamned politican : there they run to brilliantine and corsets which makes the species worse somehow. At least our types are on the tweedy side with light cologne only and let down bellies. They were around us like flies."

"What nationality?"

"Oh, the usual South American types : damned if I know one from t'other. And I kept away. The weather wasn't as good as expected, but there were plenty of days when I could bask my old bones in the sun. Did me good. But it didn't do the tour much good. Giles was abstracted half the time, leaving it to his assistant and the stage manager. Not that I ever feel at home in this cultural business, especially exporting it. The theatre is the theatre, say I, and culture for the bloody professors."

They ordered the steak and a salad.

"I thought Giles was a money sort of man," said Reed casually.

"Lucky the actor that is," said Alfred. *"Nil nisi,* but Giles had great talent. A lot of youngsters have talent. Poverty and the consequent opportunism it breeds eat it up. Oh, Giles always had money. He could tell *them* to go to hell and often did. Born with it, of course."

"There is something to being an effing juggler or conjurer," grunted Beggs. "We can always get something, even one-night stands at Masonics. Kitchen sinks never pay off !"

"We can't all be jugglers," said Alfred.

"Why not? It's practice, not even self-denial. W. C. Fields didn't deny himself if he had the money or it could be swiped, yet he practised until his palms were matted with blood. I saw it when I was his feed on the Budapest circuit in 1913. Chaplin was on some of the bills."

It would have made Beggs about eight at the time, thought Reed. In fact Beggs had probably known somebody who had fed Fields in his stupendous Budapest tour

of 1913; but this was in perfectly good theatrical tradition : stories were eventually improved by the process.
Reed had known men who, had they realised the historical
background, must have been contemporaries of the younger
Pitt.

The meal finished with good anecdotes, but little information. Everybody loved the Creams.

Reed, sober, got a cab home. By some premonition his
Austrian wife had prepared a pork goulash which above all
he loathed. Though satiated he was driven by remembered
love to eat it. Pains in his chest kept him awake night-long.

CHAPTER FOUR

THE SMALL CONFERENCE room with its little desks—as opposed to the large one which had loudspeaker systems—was crammed and Reed and Jarvis were at the same table. Reed loathed proximity when he had dried out a bit, and by some mischance the supplier had neglected to call with the beer and stout he used as a morning refresher before leaving home. There was a small coffee stall, not yet packed up—it was 8.20—where you could get a swig of brandy and Fernet Branca at this hour at double price in a greasy glass. Senior civil servants were occasionally seen doing up their shoe-laces nearby. But how to get there? He had scorned it a quarter of an hour earlier, but now it was his Holy Grail. A coup was necessary. The D.C. was reading the summary of the previous day's activities.

"I think," he said, "that we must assume that the finances of the Cream family are based, or were based, upon stolen money. Does anybody have any doubt?"

Quant led the mournful shaking of heads. A point about the old Super was that he knew when and where not to stick his wattled neck out. He had placed the D.C. in his debt. 'Endorsed by Mr Quant' would read the minute embalmed in the file.

"If I may interrupt, Commander," Reed was suave, "a thought has occurred to me, so if I may be excused . . ." He was already sidling to the door.

The D.C. was under no illusions but did not protest.

"Sergeant Jarvis," he said as the door shut.

"As instructed yesterday afternoon," said the Sergeant, "I went to see one Mr James Mark Flitch, staying at Buller's Hotel off the Strand. It is unlicensed, of a clean

74

though modest description. He occupies a single bedroom and appears to possess minimal luggage. I asked directly: 'Why did you visit Mrs Hedi Ching this afternoon?' He appeared perplexed, perhaps puzzled might be a better term. He asked 'why?' I replied that I had observed his visit while on duty and would appreciate a brief explanation."

Jarvis was not a man for the nuances of life. The assignment had been outside his experience. He had known musicians in his time, generally in connection with pot or occasionally heroin, but he could not really type the neat, shabby Flitch. A gaunt man of, say, forty-two, with what Jarvis recognised as higher education on him.

"I knew the Creams when we were kids," Flitch had said, waving the Sergeant towards the Brentwood chair and himself sitting on the end of the bed. "I've been a naturalised American since 1949. My father was one of the early brain drain lot . . . biology. But in 1940 I was evacuated to Sussex. I was in the grammar school with Peter, both of us rising thirteen, I guess. There were about four of us who used to go about together. You must know he died some years ago in a car crash."

"I'm nevertheless interested in him, sir. He became a homosexual, by the way."

Flitch had shrugged. "It is difficult to pick how anybody will develop. Peter was a strapping fellow, very blond, but not in a Nordic way. I think he had the best brain in the school. Not only did he have academic brilliance, but he was severely practical. We had the usual carpenters' shop, and I think Peter knew more than the instructors. I suppose it might have been three terms before the old manor house—let's see, Briar Heights, owned by a peer named Dockett, or something—got hit. The six Cream kids were buried for forty-eight hours."

"Did you see them afterwards?"

75

"I stayed with an uncle God knows how often removed, as they say, at Crumpiton Magnus, the little town. I remember he had an old wood-burning apparatus fixed to his car. The Creams spent a few days in hospital, not that they were more than shaken up. He drove me over. Embarrassing at that age in a way: your social awareness does not embrace hospital visits. That was the last I saw of them."

"I suppose you knew the others well?"

"No .. at that age relationships are curious. The only other one I knew was Giles, then I suppose about six. He hero-worshipped Peter and he used to tag along. A very amusing child, could mimic anything, always on the go."

"I suppose you kept in touch?"

Flitch laughed without much humour. "At thirteen relationships are evanescent, officer. No, there was nothing to keep in touch about. I stayed on with the uncle until 1945 when my father flew to the U.S. In what has seemed to me—though one surmises it does to everyone—a hard career it dawned on me that the theatrical Creams were the family I knew; that the engineering one of them who died was the Peter I knew.

"But it was just an interesting item. Eventually I took the sabbatical that I am now on, and brought my work into Ambrose's office. In fact I did not remind him that we had met until a couple of months afterwards."

"And Giles?"

"There was a liking between us," Flitch had remarked slowly. "I said, 'Hallo, Giles'. On his part it was a dim remembrance: what can you remember of people you knew when you were six?"

They—probably his grandparents—had put thirty shillings into a post office savings account, remembered Jarvis. He still had the book.

"I didn't go near him at first—just walked into Ambrose's office with my brief-case. That's business. But I've got—did

76

get—to know Giles all over again, and, *inter alia*, Mrs Ching, his mistress. A fascinating broad, if you will tolerate the expression. Giles was mad about her."

"Were they premeditating holy wedlock?" Jarvis had asked.

"I must say that when dialogue occurs in real life it is rather disturbing," said Flitch. "Wedlock! Sounds like a wrestling hold when you put it that coldly. 'The Strangler has now applied a reverse wedlock.' "

"Perhaps we could apply ourselves to the things in hand," said Jarvis primly.

"Giles and I got along. Pots of coffee and a hell of a lot of talk about the theatre. Often Hedi Ching was in it." He had hesitated, his long, Abraham Lincoln head bent, the cheap bed trembling under his weight as he moved. "I'm just an instructor in musical theory, Mr Jarvis. My horizons are pleasantly limited by academic walls. I was eighteen months in South Korea, teaching English, for Lord's sake, but then I scuttled back between these walls, such as they are now. Politicans are often amateur musicians : in fact it is a kind of fad originated by Nero and subscribed to by our contemporaries. But musicians are seldom amateur politicians—oh, I'll give you Paderewski, but a Polish politician! I am not a political animal. Hedi and Giles were."

"I'm not sure that I understand you." Jarvis wished devoutly that he was elsewhere. At work there were fat men from the London School of Economics employed to talk along those lines to suspects.

"It is obscure to me," said Flitch patiently. "Put into a nutshell, and therefore over-simplified, Mrs Ching wants to be the grey eminence of a South American Republic."

Jarvis, usually so dead-pan, felt his jaw slip.

"I know," said Flitch. "Sounds crazy, but why not? Mrs Ching is a woman avid for new sensations."

"Ah!" Jarvis felt he was coming into home water.

"Not in any brute sense," said Flitch, looking down his nose. "She would like to boss a small nation : she has economic theories one understands. Why not? It has been done before."

"U.N.O. !" said Jarvis.

"U.N.O., NATO and heart transplants," snarled Flitch, "go incant your litany elsewhere."

"That is no way to talk to an officer of the law."

"I am telling you, and I do not propose wasting my breath going over it endlessly. Giles was a romantic, an internationally known figure, and nobody suspects an actor of international intrigue. He organised a South American tour last year and met some of the big boys. . . . The C.I.A. would not necessarily oppose it. Of course . . . you see that by some mysterious process a state inhabited by illiterate peons with no ass-piece to their trousers can produce millions for their masters. Oh, I assure you that Giles and his woman were after benevolent power, not hard cash. But it did strike Giles, who was no fool, that the project might not be liked. He thought somebody might shoot him down. Nobody is easier to gun than an actor, unless a conductor, but nobody has ever bothered it seems. We're such harmless wretches ! Anyway Giles entrusted certain files to me, three in number, which I kept in that"—he indicated a battered suitcase. "Of course, one might think of a safe deposit, but not poor, romantic Giles. This morning Hedi Ching phoned me to ask if I would bring them round. I did."

"Were they papers?"

"They weighed like paper. I am not in the habit of reading other people's private documents. In any case," he gave his dry chuckle, "Giles would have insisted on code."

"Who were after him?" Jarvis adopted his most wheedling tone.

"I do not know." Flitch spoke with cold finality. "I presume, Sergeant, that this country is not entirely bereft of international information. You will surely find some person around Whitehall: or if he was killed for political reasons what about my fellow countrymen?"

Jarvis felt himself impaled. For a minute he wondered if Reed planned this, scooting off to no doubt groggy meetings with unemployed actors and leaving him to these agonising policy decisions.

"Mr Flitch," he jumped the fence, "when the Dockerns' manor house went up, something disappeared, something of value. We did wonder if Peter might have. . . ." He let the implication float, a police trick.

"Curiouser and curiouser," said Flitch. "I have no knowledge of the deed, if done. Peter was amoral, you know, but nicely so. You pushed him against a wall and he argued with you, you pushed him again and he reasoned some more. Then he looked up into the sky, your eyes followed automatically, and his knee came up into your groin. But you had to push him. If he got his own way it was all sweet. But that was so many years ago."

"On the evening of his death you saw his brother Giles?"

"I already said I was not sure. I was late. To tell you the truth," Flitch scratched his jaw, "the Creams *en masse* are rich for my blood. I'm lower middle-class and stuck there. Twelve thousand dollars is a dream year. A broken down instructor of musical theory eats ground meat. These people had broken through the money barrier and were beyond it. Giles *liked* ground meat, for Christ's sake. I saw the old lady, a proper old momma that. It was one of fifty evenings for God's sake. Ambrose had a portfolio of dialogue and the musical score in the background, very formalised, plus this mock-up on tape we were playing when you burst in."

"Came in," said the Sergeant, squiggling in his notebook.

"Call it what you cursed well like. I do not know. Sally I remember lounging in those clinging pants and getting down on the bottle. They have to practically tie her down while she's working. Joan was chomping away at rich-looking sandwiches, God knows how she does not put on weight. Dick was fussing away over stage directions—but he's clever. Ambrose, oh God, was being Ambrose, four places at once and knowing everybody's business better than they. But Giles? There was this scene with the concealed spear. All actors get fussy about a certain scene : after all they are going to appear naked in a manner of speaking. The thought of hisses makes them sweat. Dick insisted on keeping it in, he likes the heavy visual effect. I thought of an equal gag scene with poison—*mead* just imported into Rome from the barbarians. It wasn't essential, but there. . . ."

Jarvis looked up from his notebook, seeing that Reed was back in his chair.

"That is all, gentlemen."

"I must say," said Quant, with a side glance at the shorthand writer, "that one should delete the reference to Nero as a musician. It might be thought that we were looking askance at the earnest playing of church music. After all a plucking of a stringed instrument in the career of a pyromaniac"—he spelled it for the benefit of the shorthand writer—"has nothing to do with the spiritual ululations of mature statesmanship in thought at the organ of a reputable parish church."

"I must second that," said an overly ambitious inspector.

"Of course," said the D.C., thinking of his Palm Island philosophically and wondering enviously if Sergeant Reed had had a quick snort.

"Ululations?" queried the shorthand writer. Quant spelled it.

"Singing hymns must be demonstrably Right," said the over-ambitious inspector.

"We do not wish to introduce political terms," said the D.C. as a crusher. "Well, Quant?"

"Sergeant Reed endorses that there was some political activity during the South American tour and Giles was infatuated with the idea of romantic intrigue." At that moment Reed was wiping his mouth.

The D.C. made a note, somewhat wearily.

"Sir, just now I had the idea of consulting the microfilm of the old daily diary at the time of Peter Cream's fatal car crash. All that week I was working at New Malden on multiple car stealings. If I consulted the local chaps there, I might get a lead as to where the rumour that the accident was framed came from."

"Ingenious," the D.C. shrugged. "You might as well go straight out there."

He was always glad to see the back of Reed. Doubtless the fellow planned a pub crawl.

"This man Flitch," said Quant, "supposing he was demanding a share of the Dockern Treasure and Giles Cream stood in his way?"

"He looked a poorish fellow," said Jarvis, "and I can't see that he would have hugged the secret for so long."

"That tape they were playing," said the Deputy Commander, "I sent it back to Ambrose first thing this morning. But my wife and I listened to it for two hours last evening. Were I a ticket scalper I would put my modest capital into buying seats for the show without even seeing it. It had my daughters raving and made my wife laugh." Nobody present had ever seen the D.C.'s wife laugh and it was a transformation difficult to envisage. "I'm ruddy sure that the show will be a winner. That makes Flitch exactly what he says he is, an impoverished instructor in musical theory, an unknown composer and a would-be conductor who hasn't had the opportunities. This, incidentally, is what the F.B.I. say. But a point you and Reed seem to have overlooked," he looked at Quant, "is the evidence of the cook, Mrs Rumming. Her two boys, Charles and Cecil, are all bad. The husband was one of the old style bashers before somebody did him in. They were five years older than Peter. If Peter was a kid with stuff to fence, what more convenient than the cook's two sons to put him on the right track? I think he would be clever enough to handle the Rummings. They are in Brixton, by the way, waiting to give evidence in that gaol stabbing case. I will see them, also Sven-Eric Grädde, just to get it cleared away, and I will see the Fagin. Please put that clearly on record."

The D.C. paused and looked round. One of the reasons that he was so successful was that his ancestry—the members of which had always lived at the public expense—could tread delicately in spite of a generally elephantine appearance. "You will add that this unpleasant duty is nevertheless one I feel myself most fitted to perform."

The Deputy Commander had been at public school and Sandhurst with the Fagin. In the world of receivers of stolen property a kind of system of titles prevails, starting with 'Cousin Joe', progressing upwards through 'the Uncle' to 'Father'—very important indeed, but dwarfed by the throne, occupied by a gentleman known as 'the Fagin'. The nomenclature went back into the eighteen nineties when the names of Dickensian characters were common currency among the very poor and the criminals.

The current Fagin had been a strange lad at school from the day he came from Colet Court; he was the fat, unblinking scion of a pork butcher, who somehow escaped persecution and who was noted by his refusal to do anything he did not consider useful. The classics he ignored, but he was avid for economic geography and what engineering knowledge was currently supplied. Similarly at Sandhurst his interest devolved around logistics. The D.C. supposed he was that dangerous phenomenon, the Natural Crook.

"As far as the rest of you are concerned, it is quite clear

that nothing is concealed at Larchmont. Keep a man permanently there for appearance sake. But I want further interrogation of the Creams, plus appraisal of whatever property they may own. That is all."

On his way in the official Humber to see the Fagin, the D.C. thought about this successful product of society. Like so many other careers, it had got on course during 1942, about the time, he realised, that Peter Cream was getting his start.

In wartime military speculation centres around sugar. The civilian population is sugar hungry and the commodity is easily fenced. The Army cooks themselves, in peacetime followers of every non-culinary occupation, have an insatiable desire to add sugar to their greasy cooking pots. Therefore sugar disappears, or rather never appears, for the responsible officer merely signs for five tons or so of sugar which does not actually come into store. The Fagin, a rather cold-faced pudgy captain, had long known this and by 1945, when he was caught, as he knew he would be, he had accumulated two hundred thousand dollars which he had cemented under the flooring of a small country cottage he had bought under an assumed name and which was not found. The court martial dragged on for nine months one way and another, and the Fagin was cashiered and sentenced to twelve months, which meant he actually served three. By the end of 1946 the Fagin was the largest fence in Europe. He specialised in hot money and dubious 'army disposals' of metal, but he would buy anything. It was impossible to 'get' him, because the work was done by subordinates who did not mind taking seven years provided three thousand pounds clear per year mounted up in a Swiss account.

The Fagin had an office in Park Lane, partly because he was used to civilised surroundings, but more cogently because the area is more difficult to police and far more corrupt than Stepney was before the Luftwaffe erased it as a business quarter. The D.C. got V.I.P. treatment, culminating in a medically designed chair with a footrest and a good look at the receptionist's legs. He thought of native boys bringing him an iced whisky after the sun had passed the yard-arm until a deferential, tinkling voice informed him that the presence awaited.

The Fagin did not commit the solecism of offering his hand, but merely contorted his suet-pudding face into a gesture of delight and said, "my dear Brokie, what a pleasure." The D.C. had been distinguished mainly by the number of bones he had fractured at rugby football.

"Pudge, my dear soul, and how are the family?"

The Fagin was a large landlord in Devon and entertained extensively. His three sons were attending grammar schools: for the public schools of England, while welcoming free, and in fact rather competing for them, the brighter chips off the blocks of working class lags, still rigidly eschewed the sons of upper class criminals. At Oxford all would become equal again.

"Very well, Brokie, very well. The elder boy might even go into the police. I understand you are thinking of computers and that is his bent. A drink?"

"Quite frankly, Pudge, I'm after a bit of knowledge."

"Broken Hill or Mount Isa is the place to put your money long-term," said the Fagin.

"I do not mean legitimate."

"That will have to be across the board, Brokie."

"I can trade, Pudge. I want to know if the Cream family, the acting people, have fenced stolen goods."

"I'll tell you, Brokie, that in due course I might want to know where a certain person is staying for the night. You might not be able to find out. It will be forty-eight hours' notice. I assure you that no dishonesty is involved. I merely wish to protect an interest."

"If I can."

"Good enough for me. Lord, how the years roll on. About the Creams, what did you have in mind?"

"Face value, twenty-five million."

"Dear God, who swiped the Mint?"

"I would naturally consult you, my dear fellow."

"There was a Peter Cream, eldest but now dead, around 1949, who was flogging heavy stuff . . . stones. Fairly heavy. Let me think. I did not have part of it, though it was offered. I am sure that the asking price was a matter of three hundred thousand pounds : the Germans were very anxious then to trade their dollars into something durable. You can take my word for it that it was under half a million. I was heavily committed at the time : there was a syndicate who took it on, all dead now, one is afraid.

"He was a smart young fellow was Peter Cream, or so it was said. Ruthless, dynamic, would I think be the terms. But when you talk in millions, my dear fellow, you are far out. Between ourselves, nine hundred thousand pounds, and that involving gold in Hong Kong, was the largest individual transaction I ever heard of, and I had a piece of that one."

"It might have been a series of transfers," persisted the D.C.

"It was one transaction. Stones plus a few *objets d'art,* the difficult stuff to pass, museum ware. I'd have known if he was in the business."

"Did it not seem strange?"

"They were the one-shot days, remember?"

The D.C. did. The legal advisers to the underworld, not more than half a mile from Fleet Street by a quirk of poetic justice, had reflected that a dog, or a person, was allowed one bite. For some time you could earn yourself fifteen hundred pounds for being the 'front' in selling stolen property. If caught, you pleaded a blameless life, temptation from a man met in a club, and got an average of eight months. A lot of people in their late teens found it very profitable, until an amiable plot upon the part of the Establishment introduced the element of conspiracy to the charges and the handing down of six-year sentences after which it became uneconomic. All things considered, the Fagin's view was understandable.

"I'd like to help you, Brokie," said his fellow old boy, "although I may not be the fount of info I was once."

The Fagin had long ago gone into super-markets as an investment, but one of the troubles of being the Fagin was that you could never give up: while the Fagin was never betrayed, an ex-Fagin was quite often 'shopped'. He was currently working, the D.C. knew, upon the acquisition of a valid American nationalisation, though it would cost half his fortune.

"Nothing big upon the auction block, Pudge?"

"Very quiet, old fellow. I won't insult your other sources by telling you about the stealings of paintings."

"We know them," said the D.C. as he got up, gave one of the embarrassing, shuffling bows reserved for members of the criminal classes and went out to his car.

No good seeing Sven-Eric Grädde now as the man slept during the mornings, so he gave the address of the remand prison. The Rumming boys were being softened up, quite deliberately, with tastes of prime bacon-and-eggs and tailor-made tea, instead of prison slop. A taste of steak and chips and a glass of stout generally played havoc with a long-term crim's loyalty to his fellows. Two years of their sentence lopped off if they told what they saw when a fellow prisoner got a purloined screw-driver between his ribs was the offer and they were visibly weakening. The investigating officer slyly left behind girlie magazines in their double cell. Charles, the habitual spokesman for the two, a hulking man with a piping voice, said in the interview room: "We bin thinkin', sir, and perhaps we both did see a little somethink, always wishing to be of 'elp, providing we're treated fair. Reprocity as the chaplin, God bless him, sir, says of a Sunday."

"I'm not interested in the killing in the yard," said the D.C., "but in one Peter Cream."

Their faces turned blank.

"Now," said the D.C., "you keep your fancy lies for those who want them. Peter Cream's been in his grave for years. First, if you play fair with me I guarantee you four months—four months of tender girls and fried steak" (a trickle of saliva ran down Charles's scarred mouth), "off your sentence. I know that at one time he was selling large quantities of loot. I also know, from your old mum, that he became a mate of yours. I want the truth about what he flogged and where. Or—you don't know me but I am the Deputy Commander—there are certain nasty ways I have for men like you who won't do a deal. Now, you both want to start whispering, so you go and lock yourself in the carsey"—the D.C. jerked his thumb to the toilet— "for exactly ten minutes and work out just how you can fiddle me. And I'll tell you in advance that the answer is that if you do you will get down on your knees on the concrete and wish you had never been born."

Tough boys, he thought, as they got up and walked through the toilet door. He'd get them the four months off and depute Superintendent Quant to find a fresh charge carrying six months to it. He was a fair man and would allow them a week in between for the fleshpots.

He took the folded *Times* out of his jacket side pocket and read, not looking up until the piping voice said: "We'll co-operate right willing, sir, I'm sure."

The D.C. flicked his eyes over them. "Then suppose you start."

"He was a fine young fellow," said Chas.

Cecil nodded vigorously.

"I'd just as soon read the racing page as listen to your nonsense."

"He was seventeen and we were twenty-two, sir," said Chas, taking his time. "The ol' Dad had had his packet and the Mum had gone to old Mrs Cream as cook : she was in service years ago and knows fancy grub, like. We'd been in a bit of trouble because we hadn't 'eard about the Army business, not being literate, and 'adn't reported for service. But they only gave us three munce. Naturally we 'ung around Larchmont a bit, the old Mum being good for a doorstep sandwich and a coupla bob for a half pint each. One day we found Peter looking at us. He was a gent, smooth as silk, 'aving 'is last year at secondary school. I tell you that the Creams, the six of 'em, had a wild streak, Guv'nor. They 'ad a saying when we were young about 'Mayfair Boys', meaning gentlemen crooks. I did have this feelin' that the boys might get to be jool thieves and the girls 'ores in a 'igh class of business. Our Mum did say that the Grandma herself 'ad bin on the batter in 'er prime. Though I dunno. She terrified Cecil and me, the times she saw us.

"Peter got to know us. Used to slip us a packet of fags sometimes. He said he pinched them. At his age he used not to drink much, 'arf a pinta mild : he looked older than he was, a great big, fair-'aired strappin' young son-of-a-bitch, but clever with it. One day he said quite cold where could 'e find—I never have forgot the words—a moderately honest fence wot wouldn't double-cross him greatly. It was Cecil who said, 'Wot the effing 'ell?' "

Cecil was showing some sign of animation. "Or right," said his brother, "you tell it."

"It so happened," said Cecil, who dropped less aspirates, "that I did the talkin', on account that I do the fencing, like, and I knew Father Tonkin out at Notting Hill. A gentleman, sir, and never no rough stuff. A fair price and a drink to seal it all. I told young Peter and arsked 'ow much he was floggin'. Got no answer, as you might expect. He just said I was takin' a dead liberty. He offered my bruvver and me fifteen quid each to act as minders and to set the thing up.

"It was very sweet. We took him to see Father and waited outside. It took a long time for a preliminary bout, around an hour. Next day Tonkin made a point of buying us a drop. Who was this feller, he arsked. I said 'e was a promisin' young sprout of the aristocracy. Nothing happened for a week, then we took Peter back. If he carried something it was in his pockets—we'd told him that if it was portable you tried to put it in yer kick or tie it round the stummick with a bita ol' blanket. Anythin' heavy, as you know, sir, is collected by van. It was funny, though . . ." he gazed hopelessly at Chas.

"I'll take over. We was innercent then in a manner of speaking." Chas massaged scarred jowls and paid a moment's solemnity to lost innocence. "But lookin' back I often said to the bruvver, 'that was a funny thing, like'. Because Father Tonkin saw 'im the second time for four hours, and then nothin' effing 'appened, excuse my French, sir, for three effing months. Enough time to fence the Bank of England, if anybody would give you a cracker for it nowadays owin' to Labour Tyranny." He ogled the D.C. ingratiatingly.

"I vote Labour."

"Mr Wilson's a fine man, as we tell the Prison Visitors," said Chas hastily. "In three months Father Tonkin told me that he'd fixed things and the kid should come alone to a 'ouse 'e owned up Camden Town. 'E said the bruvver and me might attract attention. But Peter was bright as a button. He went and cased the place and found there was a milk bar three doors away. The appointment wiv Father was at seven, a nice respectable hour when the police relax—that's a tip I give you free, sir. So Cecil and I was to get there at six-thirty and have a bite to eat—tomato soup and canneloni it was as I remember. Peter—he had the brain, Guv'nor, 'e 'ad the noggin did that one, what a bookie 'e'd 'ave made!—said he 'ad a Device. If he threw it it made a noise like a coupla the ol' steam trains and clouds of smoke and flame like the night the ol' Crystal Palace went up. Come trouble, he'd throw it, and me and the bruvver would bash the door down and get him out and away. Wot a brain: wot a talent. Cecil and me were worried about our dough-ray-me: we were wonderin' if we could brace him, no violence, him being such a friend, for ten bob a week until it was paid off. There weren't no trouble. We follered 'im 'ome at a Discreet Interval. Two days later he came up and give us the nickers and three quid over each."

"You kept up the friendship?"

"No, sir. 'E went up to a university, and we went to college." Chas gave a small cackle. "Our first bird, sir, two years for a warehouse job."

"In which you used your boots on the watchman," said the D.C., bored with it. The two ruffians had never realised that it was Tonkin, the fence, who had slipped the vital knowledge to the local police. He wanted them 'off the street' as the saying went. "Did you ever see 'im again?"

"The ol' Mum didn't want us 'anging rahnd the 'ouse, Guy. Peter took up the cars and got hisself killed, that we read. But 'e and the others used to give the Mum a few quid for us when we was on the street."

"You do get to think in a cell, sir," said Cecil in his basso.

"I dare say," said the D.C., picking at the crossword with his little gold pencil.

"Father Tonkin got out of it a year later: we 'eard it in the gaol. I just wondered if we might have done him a rare bit of good. He wasn't more than fifty."

"You'll both get your four months off your time," said the D.C. getting up and going out the door.

'Father' Tonkin was a few lines in an old file, ruminated the D.C., back in his car. He remembered the club extensively used by retired senior officers in retirement. Personally he never intended to get near the stink of police work once he got his pension, or mercifully a job bossing natives in a sunny climate. But he went to the club, as he and others felt occasionally duty bound, and slapped six backs before buying a round.

The doyen of the establishment was a retired superintendent of detectives who had spent a few years as one of Her Majesty's superintendents of police, a rank which instils terror into Chief Constables. He had been very able : in widowed old age the years had shrunk him. His refusal to discard the old, white broadcloth 17-inch neck shirts gave his orange, wattled neck a turkey effect and his once piercing blue eyes were watery.

"I've a problem, Cuthbert," said the D.C. when they had drifted together into a corner.

"Old stuff, I guess."

"A fence called Father Tonkin."

"One of my many failures. I rather liked what I heard of him. A street bookmaker with a bit of education. He knew a lot about jewellery—it seems to go with bookmaking. As far as I could work it out he studied jewellery movements, when the stones are shifted and how. There were three or four smash-ins, probably set up by Tonkin. Then he became a fence. He was never 'in' with the Ring, a loner by disposition I judged. But he paid a little more and there was no rough stuff : a section of the trade liked him. It was getting so that I was going to put him on my special list when he dropped right out of the field. He had, let me see, a blonde little wife and two saucy daughters, lived . . . oh, damn it, my memory's going—but one day they were no longer here. A lucky one?"

"Perhaps," said the D.C. The 'lucky ones' were the boys that got out. It averaged around fifteen per cent.

"I think he got out of the country," said Cuthbert. "Noshing quid steaks in Torremolinos, most like, with a Swiss account. He must have made a big kill. I remember now that I looked into it. There hadn't been that number of big jobs the year before he scarpered. Buried treasure, no doubt!"

"Listen to this." The D.C. told him.

"I'll have another whisky on that," said Cuthbert presently. "Interpol had nothing about Tonkin. A clever fellow, no flashiness, wife and daughters shrewdies. We chose the wrong profession."

"I don't see why you stay here," said the D.C.

"I hate foreigners, lad."

"They say that in Perth, Australia, the climate is like a railway timetable before it got nationalised."

"Still foreigners. Unfortunate that it is. About Peter Cream, there was some stuff about him. A queer, you know."

"Did he blackmail?"

"Lord, no! Peter Cream always had money. I fell down on that, but it never occurred to me . . . a man with a good accent plus money is not a subject of suspicion, or was not in my day. Now perhaps it is different. I retired before he died, but he was on the List we kept in those days. Brilliant brain, I understood. They were frightened the Russians or the Americans might get at him."

"Spying?"

The old policeman shrugged. "They are always trying to get an edge on people, though so are we, not as efficiently I believe."

The D.C. talked of old times.

A memory had come back to Reed, in a sodden kind of way. It was something to do with a pub and a rather frightened youth. He parked his Aston Martin D.B.S. outside the local station and to his surprise a chief inspector recognised him.

"It's been a long time since we had a pint in the Bunch of Grapes, Mr Reed."

"It is that," said the Sergeant cautiously.

"It was the day I'd been made senior constable, which is why I remember it, and we were after a young thief named Nicholas. We thought he was driving for a car gang. Reason why I remember it was that two years later I arrested him for murdering an aged lady. It was under the old law and he was topped. Only time I've ever had a murder case, as the ball bounces. But you and I had a game of darts with him and you missed double thirteen twice."

"I'm no good on double thirteen," said Reed, remembering a little more. "Was there a bit about Peter Cream?"

"The old fellow," said the Chief Inspector, "Lord what a memory you have got, Mr Reed! Old Teddy Gold it was, nattering away about it. I saw you prick up your ears. He's been dead, oh, Lord knows how many years. He said that Peter had been got at, though the Ministry Inspector found nothing. An old fool, drink in, brains out, but you took a note. You had just got your sergeancy, I believe, and young and ambitious like all of us."

He had, Reed realised, a streak of the petty malice that police work tended to breed into you.

"Wasn't he an old mechanic?"

The Chief Inspector caressed a fleshy, pimpled snout. "He has a son who has bettered himself. Old Teddy was on the production line all his life, young Ted has a panel beating shop. He does any work we have. Good, solid bloke. About half a mile away."

He watched Reed go. He knew all about the Sergeant and was careful to write in his diary, divided into quarter-hours, 'when leaving appeared in full possession of his faculties'.

Reed parked his car outside a trim workshop. A middle-aged man was looking sadly at a dented car.

"I met your late father years ago," said Reed, plunging into it. "I'm Sergeant Reed, C.I.D."

"I'll be damned. The old chap died four years ago."

"He thought Peter Cream had been got at."

Green eyes looked at Reed for a moment. "If you'd been interested it's ten years too late."

"They say murder will out."

Gold looked at his big, work-scarred hands. "The old man was seventy-seven when Peter bought it. I've got all the trade school qualifications that he had not got, but as a practical mechanic I'm not his left boot-lace. He belonged to the generation which got hold of some metal and in eight months produced a car which is still running. That's the background. I only saw Cream but once. A big, blond, smiling kind of bloke who I disliked. Class consciousness, I think, though he might have been a phoney. Dad used to putter around for him. If you had a carburettor problem you couldn't do better than let Dad muck around with it. Or a lot of other things. It gave Mum and Dad a drop of whisky and a cut of salmon when they wanted it. Nothing mean about Cream. Now my Dad had perfect vision nearly to the last, and I mean perfect. For his birthday I'd given him one of those fancy binoculars that fit like glasses and are good for watching moving objects. He used to like to stand on a bridge or a hill and watch cars. Poor old bugger! The morning Cream got it he was watching intently. Now," Gold talked carefully, "he said that someone had slackened off the ball joint at one end of the track rod. Do you understand . . . ?"

"Yeah," said Reed, "you corner at upwards of eighty and you go off the road right smart."

"That is what the old bloke said. He used to boss a pit at Brooklands in the year dot and he had seen it happen. The tail starts to waggle and you've just got time for a very short prayer. I'd take his word, but he was seventy-seven when they'll trust you politically but not mechanically."

94

"You could get a boy not tightening the joint."

"Not the team that Cream kept. They were seasoned mechanics like my Dad. At the inquest the work sheets proved the routine inspections had been made. You couldn't check the remains, tomato purée and molten metal."

"I suppose it *was* Cream who was behind the wheel?" an uneasy thought struck Reed.

"The old man spoke to him after the motor fired." Gold looked at him curiously. "He said, 'I think we've got a good one here' and Peter flapped his hand. Lord, when his brain started to suffer, I heard the story five hundred times. I wish I could hear it another five hundred. We told all this to Miss Gocher."

"Who?"

"I must say it's the only time I saw a Private Eye. Not that she may not have eyes under the dark glasses. Little mouse lady with a scarf over her head! My Mum liked her : they exchanged recipes. Dad told what he knew."

"Thanks," said Reed. "I'm afraid it was just a routine report." Just in case there was a murder around you kept it cool.

He knew Miss Gocher quite well. The name was pronounced Gocker and she was a widowed grandma of astute propensities who had recently transferred her business to Guildford because of the adultery. He drove slowly and arrived there at noon. In her sere years Nellie Gocher had a largish and competent staff and had given up the factory jobs to concentrate entirely on double beds.

"Reed," she said, in her chintzy office which had persuaded so many outraged spouses to take the irrevocable step, "how nice to see you! Are you still on the sherbert?"

He licked parched lips as Miss Gocher mixed a very dry martini as a matter of course.

"Nellie," he said after the first gulp, "do you remember seeing an old mechanic named Ted Gold about the death in a car of one Peter Cream?"

Miss Gocher nearly speared her thumb on the half-opened tin of olives.

"Dear me"—she never swore, rare in her profession—"the only time I could have made like Pete Chambers! The only case of violence I ever had except thrashing women which is normal and you can't hardly ever get a conviction for."

"Look, Nellie, when I was a young constable . . ."

"I know"—Nellie was drinking straight gin, realised the Sergeant—"never interfere between man and woman, though it's her that gets kicked in the slats."

"Keep to the rails, Nellie."

"Peter Cream had a gran. She must be pushing ninety, now. No flies on, nasty if in a corner."

Reed looked at her with respect. "She hired you?"

"Yeah. Grand dame stuff. I was working off the Gray's Inn Road when I got the summons. A mechanic—look it up if you want—had phoned her. She'd heard about me regarding divorce, or rather, I must say, my grandfather who started the business. He was a disbarred solicitor who arranged the fancy Edwardian dirt. There was a shortage of staff in those days. She goes back a long time. The pre-pre-pre international set, God bless their stove pipe trousers and frilly drawers! But the case," she drank a little gin, "was nowt. There was a Ministry man at the inquest. Everything had been busted or fried, no physical evidence except that the pit team swore they had checked things out okay, but they *would*. I put a couple of smartish men on it—no soap. I strung Mrs Cream along for twelve days and gave her a negative and the bill. A matter of a hundred odd quid in those days. She paid : file closed."

She mixed another martini in the shaker. Reed lay back in the Windsor chair and drank and ate olives. After the fifth glass he snored.

Miss Gocher's thumb banged a bell. Her two sons entered, small, bright and intelligent men. She got a pin from a small box on the surface of the desk and jabbed Reed an inch under his right eye. There was no twitch.

"Pissed," she said clinically. "Give him a nice lie-down."

There was a room with a bed where operatives, awaiting call, could take a snooze. Her sons laid the Sergeant on the bed.

"This Cream thing," said their mother, "another one got killed as you may have noted. They say where that drunk Reed works there is always the stink of money. I want you lads to get out to the garage and go through the old files. There's a chance we can screw something out of this one. I smelled something at the time: couldn't locate the precise whiff."

"Yes, Mum."

Sergeant Reed, his head poked out of the bedroom into the communal hallway, gently withdrew it and closed the door.

"Herr Grädde?"

The secretary was young and had a scrubbed look. Herr Grädde occupied six rooms and was wearing trousers and a singlet, for which he apologised to the D.C.

That he had got in, realised the latter, was entirely due to the Swedish preoccupation with pecking order: he had presented the card he carried with the courtesy title of 'Honourable' engraved on it. The fourth child of a bankrupt baron deserves small privileges.

"Do sit down Commander," said Grädde. "I have this habit of sleeping by day. You will join me in something?"

"I like Swedish odds and ends. Eminently civilised. And I have not eaten. The curse of our profession is dyspepsia."

"We will try to cure it." There was an atmosphere of scurrying until ample coffee and loaded plates were respectfully put within reach.

Herr Grädde, who looked as though he could eat like several horses, dutifully discussed dyspepsia and the therapeutic merits of yoghurt.

"I operate more or less on a committee basis, Herr Grädde," said the D.C. as he gathered up a smoked-pork sandwich.

"That is endemic nowadays," agreed Grädde, picking up a sliver of pickled fish like a chess master replying to a gambit.

"They wondered why you should have been carrying a torch around the night Giles Cream was killed. You did not set out with the intention of visiting Larchmont, or that was my understanding."

"I must admit that I was somewhat less than frank," said Grädde. "In my mind was the possibility that I might try to have a word with one of the Creams, Giles to be exact. I say possibility quite advisedly : I was hesitating." His blue eyes looked at the D.C. "I have known the Creams for many years, to be exact since 1948. I am of course considerably older. As usual one has a favourite. In my case it was young Giles, a mercurial child when first I saw him. I watched his career." He gave something between a sigh and a small groan. "This scheme we have, it was probable that my old acquaintanceship was why I was approached. . . . There are often personal considerations in business. Not that it is sentiment : it should be a good operation, and it suits me and the others to hedge some money into entertainment. People always wish to be amused, however bankrupt the economy. I . . ."—he interlocked his long, sturdy fingers—"came to suspect that all might not be above board. I trusted Giles : the other Creams are very clever people. I could not say that I believed in them implicitly."

"What kind of funny business?" asked the D.C., as he helped himself to smoked swordfish.

98

"It was a question of the assets which they were putting in," said Grädde. "They own six theatre leases."

The D.C. ogled a small, deliciously ripe tomato stuffed with chopped crayfish meat and cream sauce, reluctantly abandoned his assault on it in favour of partridge in escabeche sauce. "I suppose you chaps get a valuation," he said.

"There was a valuation," said Grädde, "but my fellows thought it might have been fiddled. There are other things as well. You see we like to sterilise things, my associates and I. We do not want to start off by demanding independent appraisals : thereafter all would be distrust and eventual law-suits. I was wondering how I could have a quiet word to Giles so that it was all revised agreeably and with no one losing face."

He really should lose the ten pounds his doctor was harping on, thought the D.C. and pushed his plate away after mopping up the sauce with the crisp remainder of his roll.

"You left this suite at what time?"

"A quarter to eleven at night. I had been working with my secretary."

Nothing to it, thought the D.C.

"If there was funny business and Giles might be the weak link would not his relatives have a valid reason to kill him?"

"They are not a family like that," said Grädde stiffly.

He meant that monied people do not kill each other, thought the D.C. He said : "Did you ever wonder where the Creams got their money from?"

"The grandmama, of course."

"She has had under two thousand a year gross since the nineteen-twenties."

Grädde's eyes were goggling. "But that is impossible. They were wealthy young people."

"I assure you," said the D.C., "that as far as old Mrs

99

Cream is concerned my information is impeccable. To put it quite frankly, which I only do because you are a money-man on an international scale and understand the gravity of these things, we believe that Peter Cream, the one who died, master-minded the theft of a great deal of loot in the shape of jewellery."

"You will excuse me, but that I cannot believe. The good grandmama, the brilliant children. . . ."

"Where did they get their money when they were starting?"

"It is unusual for me to drink at this hour," said Grädde, "but you will join me in a small brandy?"

"A good idea."

"Paul!" The secretary, white-faced, young and bespectacled, utterly discreet the D.C. supposed, scurried to get a bottle. It was a brand that the D.C. could not afford and was not likely to.

"I am stupified," said the Swede as more coffee was poured. "To think that I am on the brink of dealing with crooks. Oh, I accept your professional advice."

"It is not quite that," said the D.C. warily. "I said *Peter* Cream, who is dead. I make no, repeat no, allegations regarding the rest of the family."

"That is understood." Grädde took up a memorandum pad and scribbled momentarily. "Neither of us make libellous allegations, no?"

"We are on the same course."

"They always had money," said Grädde. "I believed from the grandmama. She knew wealthy men, perhaps you know?"

"We know all about the grannie. She did all right, but not millionaire stuff."

"They have always had money," said Grädde. "You will understand that in my position I am always being asked for money. One gets so wary of the situation and the unpleasantness of it. They always had money. This is so curious.

I have helped them: one always wishes to use other people's money and my introductions helped. But they did not come as supplicants which is the main thing when one wants to borrow. It is perhaps strange, but my own father always told me, 'never lend a poor man money'. His father told him it."

"Quite!" The D.C. absent-mindedly allowed the secretary to refill his glass and thought of the eight hundred and fifty pounds an indigent niece wanted to borrow on the strength of a badly built apartment. "Quite! But how did you come to know the Creams?"

"Through my dear mother," said Sven-Erik Grädde, "who knew old Mrs Cream. A remarkable lady that, though in her generation that sort of lady was often socially acceptable. My mother was English."

A ducal family, remembered the D.C. "I am aware of that," he said.

"During the war she bethought herself of Mrs Cream. Through our American connection we sent food parcels: and I think we perhaps eased her in other ways, clothes through the Embassy, that sort of thing. Our hearts were in the right place as you know."

"Yes," said the D.C. without much enthusiasm.

"It was not until 1947 that I had time to visit them: and somewhat to my astonishment found such a charming, prosperous family."

"How often did you see them?"

Grädde shrugged. "When we coincided. It could be anywhere with the Cream children from Europe to South America. The old grandmama only goes to Cheltenham once a year. I know many of the international set, if you care for the term. My two wives were, and are actresses. We are on good, divorced terms." He shrugged. "It is useful for the business: the yacht and the beautiful people. Oh, God!" He roared with laughter. "Beauty does lie in the eye of the cheque book, Commander, in so many cases,

101

but the Creams are beautiful physically. Beauty and money, my dear fellow, what a valuable combination and how rare. They were, they are, in demand by everybody. Yet, in case I have misled you in any way, I must emphasise that apart from my current disagreement—and that perhaps a technicality—they are just charming guests. You want this in writing?"

"I don't think so, Herr Grädde. It will be the question of plodding on. We will win, of course, because we have the apparatus. It is a strange case. He threw himself down on this spear, believing it to be a rubber mock-up. It was high-grade steel."

"I do not think he was the kind of man to suicide."

"That is hardly the picture I formed," said the D.C., wishing he had not had so much to eat and reluctantly coming to the conclusion that smoked foods played hell with his stomach lining. "He seemed to enjoy life. Everything to live for, etcetera, as far as we know. There had been some talk of political ambition."

"Buying a banana republic?" Grädde smiled. "Even our American friends have tired of that pursuit. However, given money, you can play heavy politics around the Latin countries. He would have tired of it : the food is very bad for northern stomachs and the women all the same. Sweaty!"

"Could you get killed?"

Grädde's broad face momentarily hardened, the blue eyes assuming a doll-like glassiness. "Of course, my dear fellow, one's interests do take in the periphery of armaments. You can, if you dabble politically instead of doing the sensible thing of bribing the chief-of-staff at their revolting war offices, get shot down. But Giles Cream? Had he weight enough? I have a man who knows about such things, perhaps," he smiled, "on a lower level than the diplomats. I will get a reply from him by tomorrow."

The Deputy Commissioner shook hands and left. The

deep carpeted corridor was empty. He snapped open his cigarette case which doubled as a listening device. Two small rubber cups pinned it to the door, a thin strand of wire culminated in a plug which fitted in his large red ear hole. At a distance he looked like a man who had just closed a door. If the door opened the case would drop into his hand and he would give a polite nod and make his way to the lift. The magnification was tremendous.

"Paul," Grädde spoke English.

"Sir?"

"Get my man in B.A. I do not wish to be directly concerned. A Giles Cream has been murdered. Was it South American politics? If so, who? There will be a handsome bonus for him."

"Yes, sir."

Along the corridor a lift door clicked, and the D.C. took the cigarette case into his hand as a spring coiled up the wire. He strolled along the corridor to where the lift waited.

Sergeant Reed was generally in favour of the siesta principle: a bellyful of grog and a snore-off in safety seemed to him to be the better part of Latin civilisation. In particular the bedroom in which he was luxuriating had got a plumbed wash-bowl which Latin civilisations had not. He had removed the elastic-sided shoes that drink had reduced him to and periodically recovered consciousness long enough to open the door a crack and listen.

He was apparently asleep three hours later when Miss Gocher entered with a breathalyser.

"Come on, my dear, and see whether we can drive."

Reed expelled breath.

"Fine, my love," said Miss Gocher. "Completely sober

are we, so now perhaps you might drive off, work having to be done. Put on your boots now."

"Ta, my sweet, ta ever so," said Reed as he obliged and walked ponderously out of the house. He drove for a mile and adeptly parked in a side street. It was old stuff for him and should have been for Miss Gocher and her two sons, but the thought of extortion caused them to drive blithely past. Reed grinned and drove to the nearest telephone box. On his authority the police guard on Larchmont faded into the background. When he arrived there the nondescript Triumph used by the Gochers was parked at a discreet distance from the house. He made no effort of concealment and a plainclothes constable trotted smartly up from round the corner.

"I have a front door key, Mr Reed."

The Sergeant went in. Inside the long hallway were crouched, in pecking order, the housekeeper, Mrs Rumming and the companion, Miss Birch. Avarice lit their faces.

"Now, my old chum," came Miss Gocher's voice from the breakfast room, "you are in trouble and you can trust me. It's merely a matter of money."

Reed opened the door and leered slyly round. The elder of the Gocher sons indiscreetly came forward fast and collapsed on the ground, retching.

"I think your son has had a fit, Miss Gocher," said the Sergeant politely. "Do you wish me to summon medical help?"

"You effing bastard," said Miss Gocher. Her son struggled painfully to his feet.

"You will find the brandy inside that small cupboard," said old Mrs Cream with stage majesty, "and for ourselves alone. The company is low, but you will find the brandy good. An old admirer instructed his estate to send me a dozen a year. He died in 1913."

"You old whore," said Miss Gocher.

"A successful old whore," said Mrs Cream, without passion, "who may out of the kindness of her heart visit you at Holloway Gaol."

"Extortion!" said the Sergeant, pouring two small ones.

"You dare not prefer a charge," said Miss Gocher.

"In fact, my dear," said Mrs Cream, "you will not find me ungenerous to the extent of a couple of hundred pounds. The two thousand you demanded is unreasonable."

"Take it, ma," said the younger son.

"Cash," said Miss Gocher, ignoring her elder boy's venomous leers.

"I always keep a few hundred in the sideboard," said old Mrs Cream. "Mr um, Policeman, will get it."

It was behind the liquor bottles. Seven hundred nicker, estimated Reed as he counted two hundred out and returned the rest. His pudgy hand snaked down and pinioned Miss Gocher's outstretched skinny one. "But info included, my loving soul."

"Your Peter was killed all right," said Miss Gocher with gusto.

Mrs Cream rocked to and fro, but her curiously unlined face was impassive.

"Facts," said Reed.

"It stank," said Miss Gocher. "There was an old mechanic who said the front end had been got at. I saw him myself. Funny business!"

"You did not tell me that at the time," said Mrs Cream.

"How could I? An old mechanic. It was just my smeller that told me."

"That's not enough."

"Peter was a well-known Gay," said Miss Gocher sullenly. "The Boys around the West End knew him. I keep a list of them, or did before they changed the Act."

"You cannot blackmail 'em now," said Reed, "which is one reason why you transferred to Guildford."

"I must say that in my day," said Mrs Cream, "it was disapproved of, though one must admit they were witty."

The old lady had a tendency to wander, thought Reed. Aloud he said : "There was some business about a key."

"On his death bed," intoned Miss Gocher, "he went on about it. It was delivered to the second eldest, Ambrose. A good key—I got a sight of it by bribing the hospital porter. I thought he'd been fiddling the taxation and it was a deposit box."

There was a slight scuffling noise outside the door which opened.

"Unhand me," camped Miss Sally Cream. "This is molestation."

"Leave my sister be, the bitch," said Dick Cream. "What has she been a-doing of?"

"You have no ear for dialogue," said Sally.

"They forced their way in," said the sweating constable. "I do not wish to say anything against the lady, but, speaking as a married man, she did thrust her bosom out and kind of push me aside."

"Stick to beer and you will have no trouble," advised Reed, "and go back to your post."

"Pour another round of drink," said Mrs Cream.

"Assaulting a constable is seriously looked upon," said Reed as he poured.

"But I assaulted him in the nicest possible way." Miss Cream lacked the slight angularity of the rest of the family and had two dimples.

"To come to the point," said Dick, adding ginger ale to his glass, "have you made a ruddy arrest? This thing is not doing us any good. And do not think I am callous : in a way I'm speaking for Giles, too. And Peter, God rest him."

"There was a key," said Reed. "On his death bed Peter worried about it. It was given to Ambrose."

"I can vouch for that," said Miss Gocher, her face sharp.

"And you can now take your two boys and vouch off before I think up a holding charge," said Reed.

He watched through the window until he saw them drive off.

"I think," said Dick Cream, "that we should have Joan and Ambrose, plus Howe, our solicitor. I will phone if it is okay."

"I shall have to telephone," said Reed. "I suppose it concerns the Dockern loot."

"My God," said Sally Cream, "do you . . ."

"Don't say anything, kiddo," said Dick, "until we have a lawyer."

The old lady sat silent as Reed and Dick Cream went out to the telephone.

CHAPTER FIVE

THEY WERE BACK in old Mrs Cream's drawing room. She had climbed on to the red plush seat of her ornate commode. The Deputy Commander was in a Windsor chair, with Superintendent Quant taking the shorthand note. Not too usual, but Reed had had a certain leering triumph in his voice when he had counselled discretion. "Very softly, sir, to catch these particular monkeys."

Sally Cream was a dish, thought the D.C., looking sourly at her legs. Lady Cynthia, in her remote prime never disported such gams. Dick sat near her, his butter-coloured hair symmetrically parted. Ambrose, his face drawn, sat near Joan, who chain smoked. The lawyer, Howe, looked immensely assured. Sergeant Reed, in the corner, had a glass in his hand. It riled the D.C., but Reed had *sotto voce* reminded him instructions had been to lush the old lady.

"I understand you may wish to make a statement regarding a certain key, possibly connected with the Dockern hoard."

"I think Miss Gocher deduced something on these lines," said Reed.

"She is just an ordinary blackmailer," said old Mrs Cream. "She thought I was vulnerable and was right. Anybody with a family is. In my young days I assure you that practically everybody in London had to pay, one way or another."

"Not to dance about," said the D.C., smiling fatly, "there was a treasure, loot worth five millions at that time, lifted from the Dockern house when it got blown."

"Me and Giles," said Sally Cream. "We took it home in our suitcases."

"I must warn you . . ."

"We were seven years old," said Sally.

"My God," said the D.C.

"In 1941 no child under eight could commit a crime— since 1963 the age is ten and it will shortly be put up. Therefore the two children under eight do not appear to be guilty of any crime unless they had any stones left after January first, 1969, when the Theft Act (1968) came into force." Howe was plainly enjoying himself. "If they had— and we can prove they had not—they could then be guilty of theft or dishonest handling because the rule that there had to be *animus furandi* at the time has gone. Children under fourteen can rely in any proceedings upon very strong presumption of their innocence. But they are legally capable of committing crimes although a knowledge that they were doing wrong would have to be proved. In this case it was the two seven-year-olds who did the crime."

"But in after years they came of age," spluttered the D.C.

"No doubt you will consult the Crown Solicitor, sir," said Howe with unction, "as to whether a legal adult is bound to confess to a crime committed as an unprosecutable minor? His reply might be interesting."

"It was Treasure Trove and should have been reported to a Coroner," said Quant. "Five millions, in those days, of gems!"

Howe placed his fingertips together. "The stones are not Treasure Trove which is only gold and silver in coin, plate or bullion. Treasure Trove is in fact precious metal hidden or lost by the owner with the intention of *reclaiming* it. It belongs to the Crown. However, if deliberately *abandoned* by the owner, it belongs to the first finder. I admit that the gems under discussion do not belong to the latter category.

They were probably *bona vacantia*; in other words, though not Treasure Trove they belong to the Crown. Therefore I admit they are legally capable of being stolen—which Treasure Trove is not, the possible offence being concealment—as they do have an owner."

"Exactly, an offence, to wit theft, was carried out."

"Legally, perhaps, but a child under eight can do no wrong. It seems to me," said Mr Howe, "that your arguments are mutually exclusive."

Like an old, but snappy tortoise Quant hunched and prepared for fresh attack. The D.C., who had been wondering why his horsey daughters had not thought of felony at an early age, the stupid bitches, intervened.

"The key," he said.

"It seems to me, without making any admissions," said Ambrose Cream, "that there was a door, leading off the cellar where we had our bomb shelter and that Peter made a key to it. He was very proud of it. It was a complicated apparatus, though one would not imagine that an ordinary burglar could have penetrated to what one remembers as the dark, gloomy reaches of that old house."

"No ordinary burglar," said Sally Cream.

"But you all knew," said Quant.

"That will be denied," said the lawyer. "Are you proposing to cross-examine adults as to what they did as children?"

The D.C. met Sergeant Reed's bibulous, knowing eye and gained a message. "I suppose it just might be a question of restitution," he said.

Joan Cream rolled her eyes at the ceiling.

"I should say that I've been a stupid old woman," said Mrs Cream, her voice ominous. "It is not nice to find one has been deceived by one's grandchildren. At my age it does not matter. I assure you I knew nothing of the matter, though the acquisitive streak must run in their blood. . . . I shall indicate my displeasure, of that I assure you." Her face could become very cold, noted the D.C.

"Gran," said Ambrose, placating.

"Shut your stupid mouth."

"Commander," said Howe, "can I tell you a little story?"

"I think your profession is a minor branch of fiction," said the D.C. without real humour in his voice.

"Suppose Peter Cream, a man of devious thinking—I just about knew him myself—and a Marxist by conviction, took only a half a million of the Dockern jewellery and fenced it for half that amount. A tidy sum in the fifties."

"Oh, Jesus," implored the D.C., privately praying for the smallest available sinecure, acceptable to his wife, outside England.

"The rest he put into a suitcase and dropped it in the Kennet-Avon Canal, preserving a map of the spot."

"Half a million was missing," growled Quant, "worth two and a half million pounds today."

"And twenty-odd million to be retrieved—if the story was true," said Howe. "Sunk in Wiltshire mud, of course, but jewels do not rot."

"I do not know whether we can compound," said the D.C.

"What have you to compound? Hearsay? Miss Sally Cream has admitted complicity to a crime committed when she could not commit one. She will not admit any knowledge of Peter's handling of the results. If you wish to push it, nothing will be admitted and our discussion here will be as if it never existed."

"I'll have to think of it," said the D.C.

"You will have to make a certain decision here and now. My view is that the financial state of the country is not so sound as to permit a wilful turning down of money."

The D.C. wished he could turn the decision over to Reed who had rolled his eyes again. He thought it meant, "yes".

"My dear sir," he said, "you are surely in no position to deny sound legal deliberation." Beautiful legal pickings in the offing, he thought, watching the lawyer's face.

"Well," said Howe ". . ."

"Well, nothing," said Ambrose Cream, "as my sister was then a minor and penniless she would apply for free legal aid. Tell that to your Treasury friends. It would go to the House of Lords on appeal if you tried to proceed against her."

The D.C. looked at his brown, mottled hands and thought of having natives birched. He was sure that those areas administered by the Metropolitan Police still had salutary methods of enforcing law and order. A good police sergeant to administer it perhaps. There would of course be native lawyers, but these surely could be squared. Aloud he made his gamble.

"I dare say," he said, "that if a substantial amount was recovered, and viewing the circumstances as outlined, no charges would be offered."

"That is handsome of you," said Howe, a trifle reluctantly.

"I'll tell you this," said Ambrose Cream. "There is no money to be had from us personally in this matter. Have your legal fun if you wish : the tax-payer foots the bill for less amusing capers."

"Where was it?" asked Quant, matter-of-factly.

"One understands there may be a map," said Joan Cream, pushing back her blonde hair, "indicating that Peter may have deposited something off a lock near Devizes. He went down and spent the night, when he was eighteen, at The Bear. I know nothing of it."

"Hypothetically, and not for any kind of record," said the D.C., "you are telling me that Peter, Marxist by nature, decided to keep a half a million of the loot and dropped the remainder in the canal."

"I always worked hard for my money," said old Mrs Cream severely. "It was only right. Many a wallet I could have gone through but disdained such a practice."

"Times change, Grannie, my love," said Sally Cream, "besides which the gentlemen only carry Diner's Club cards these days."

The old lady laughed. "Children!"

"This key," said the D.C. doggedly, "was a symbol, was it not?"

"It was a secret between us all," said Dick, "We were very young. It was a kind of game with us. Peter carried the key: it was a 'thing'. He used to pull the key-ring out and grin at us. We used to giggle."

"Because you knew a crime had been committed," said the D.C.

"We are not progressing anywhere," said Ambrose, equally cold.

"Indeed I am afraid not," said the lawyer. "By dint of some dredging device you may well recover a King's Ransom, rather more in view of the way the market has been going in royalty. I would rest on your laurels."

"But Giles was killed," said old Mrs Cream.

"We have got away from the important point," said Sergeant Reed, his glass refilled. "As we are speaking off the record it was a quarter of a million obtained for the loot that got you started?"

"I would not put it that way," said Howe. "For the record we deny it."

"Understood, but Peter and Giles were probably murdered, Giles almost certainly. We have to ascertain whether the motive rests among this old crime, record or no record. The Commander is not compounding murder."

"Sergeant," said Joan Cream, "I was next to Peter in age, so I may speak for us. We *were* a united family. We *are* a united family. The question of murder among us is quite out of the question. Our relationship had, has ceased to be personal, in that we have long ago accepted each other's idiosyncracies. Our relationship is intellectual, apart from the catalyst of Grannie."

113

"I'm talking about money," said the Sergeant, unimpressed. "All this psycho business goes out of the window where there's money or sex. I'm speaking as an old copper."

"There was never any trouble between them," said Mrs Cream with finality.

"Somebody," said the D.C., "with sufficient knowledge of the plot of this play, with knowledge that Giles was fussing over the production bit, went up to that room and substituted a lethal weapon for the rubber prop. The original mock-up had been in the room for a week. Who did the substitution?"

Quant had crept to the door and now whipped it open. Miss Birch and Mrs Rumming almost fell in.

"As you have heard most of it, ladies," said Quant, "have ye comments?"

"Nobody would have wished to kill Mr Giles I'm sure," said Miss Birch. Reed recognised a certain palpable, greedy falseness. Another two quid a week would be requested on the morrow. You had to put on the other side of the scales that the wealthy are always hated by their servants, and domestic servants hate more than most.

"A lot of people always in the 'ouse," said Mrs Rumming, practically. "And the room in which poor Mr Giles passed over was never cleaned often. I 'ave an agreement with the mistress about the cleaning. Six rooms are done regular, or at least fairly regular, but the rooms for re'earsal and storage get a light tickle once every six munce, which makes the next at Christmas. Theatricals, sir, and with all due respect I'm sure, are honnaccountable, rilly. It's the 'ard and 'arsh light they work under what slightly affects the 'ead after many years at it so they say." She leered and nodded at the Creams.

The D.C. had of late found himself increasingly wishing that he had the power to order the immediate execution of certain people and he thought it now.

"Giles had certain political affiliations," suggested the D.C. "I suppose you know about his lady?" said Ambrose.

"Mrs Hedi Ching? We do know," said the D.C.

"She has political ambitions," said Ambrose. "I only know because as a united family we have had to keep an eye on the others. It is a difficult equation to present to strangers."

"I understand," said the D.C., thinking of three hundred pounds he had lent to a maternal aunt in 1959 who still owed it. "But I would like to hear more."

Ambrose shrugged. "I might make my position clear. I do not care anything about politics. We could earn more if we were Russian citizens in terms of material possessions."

Dear God, thought the D.C. Aloud he said, "You must realise, my dear sir, that the Metropolitan Police are strictly non-political. We know that *these things happen* but we try to take a broad-minded, a permissive attitude within the structure of our great democracy."

Quant busily wrote it into his book against the possibility of an enquiry from above.

Joan said, sulkily, "There was some kind of intrigue. The Ching woman is reputedly always looking for kicks. There was a man named Pidal, a South American, who had threatened Giles. He did not take it too seriously. He was a very powerful, fit man who knew judo. We hoped Giles would forget it all : he'd had a thing about Ching for long enough. He always suddenly tired of his women."

"Humph," said the D.C. "Could anybody get into this house during the day?"

Mrs Cream looked at the back door. "Sometimes I do forget to fasten that back door. At 1.30 each afternoon I go to my bedroom and sleep for exactly one hour. Miss Birch does the same in one of the upstairs rooms. Rumming seats herself in the kitchen with the door shut watching the TV she has there. So, you see?"

"The spear could be carried under a light coat easily,"

ruminated the D.C., "but it would have to be somebody known here."

"I don't see . . ." Dick started and stopped.

"One, because he knew the house. Two, because if a total stranger *had* been seen there would have been an uproar so he or she must be accepted into the house. Three, the murderer knew all about the business of the spear and Giles' intention to rehearse it."

"While this house is family," said Ambrose, "I suppose dozens of people have come to see us here over the years. As for the spear business, I gave one of your men a list of thirty people who knew about that piece of business."

"It does seem to me that Herr Grädde barged in suspiciously," said Reed.

Mrs Cream laughed slightly. "I knew his father : one of the wealthiest men in Europe and certainly the meanest."

"Well, thanks very much," said the D.C. "Now perhaps I may have that map."

CHAPTER SIX

FIVE HOURS LATER Reed and 'Crying' Jarvis were in the billards room of a broken-down little old hotel in the shabbiest part of Soho. It was known simply as 'Dupont's' and went back a hundred and twenty years so the ancient smells of garlic and cheap oil were imbedded into the woodwork. Yet some kinds of foreign men—women were not taken—found it useful, regularly dining at the long tables with stained tablecloths. At this place a South American named Pidal had a small room. Jarvis who could get along in Spanish and French was noted for his contacts among the seamier foreign communities. Pidal might possibly have been at a grade one hotel, but there is a separate squad which covers them and they had never heard of the name. So they had gone to Reed's flat, which was nearest, and relaxed comfortably while Jarvis, thumbing a green notebook, had made a hundred-odd telephone calls : rooming houses, odd little cafés, places which provided gambling, ladies or drugs.

"Sorry," he said at length, "but I just did not think of Dupont's. It is so near the bottom of the barrel, and 'sides they have mostly French and Belgians. Señor Pidal might be a clever one."

"Never been in Dupont's," said Reed, sipping cold beer at the rate of a quart every forty minutes, what he called not drinking but a steady teetotal trot.

"A fleabag! There's a combination desk clerk, billiards marker and whatnot, he might even own it, who is under an obligation to me. Pidal has been there six weeks. A squat powerful fellow."

"Got handcuffs?"

Jarvis, who had handcuffing to a fine art, nodded. "Pidal comes in at ten, never fails."

In an hour they moved off, Mrs Reed having provided omelettes and a large, sticky sweet.

The desk-clerk-cum-billiards-marker was a lugubrious Frenchman with a nose which a great deal of drink had gone to produce. The advantage of the room with its two patched tables was that you could see the first floor landing, in one of the rooms off which Pidal stayed. The marker limped off with Reed's pound note to the pub down the way and returned with two quart bottles of beer, a glass and a double brandy for himself. At five to ten Reed put down his glass.

"He comes now." The marker's nose turned towards the half open door as he listened to the steps. Pidal was indeed a squat man. They could see the rolls of fat at the back of his neck as Reed stepped behind the door and held one arm with Jarvis a step behind.

"Policia" shouted Jarvis and Pidal froze before turning very slowly. Then his hand whipped upwards, but Reed chopped him with paralysing force over the biceps. Jarvis's big hand slipped into the breast of the forty-guinea brown suit and came out with a small revolver, a four shot job.

"Dear me," said Reed. "Have you a licence, Mr Pidal?"

"You know I have not." His English was perfect apart from its slight sing-song and softness. "For the record I carry it to protect myself. There are bad fellows who dislike me."

Jarvis had pocketed the gun and quietly slipped one handcuff over Pidal's right wrist and put the other on his left. Outside, their taxi was waiting at the taxpayer's expense. They drove to the local station.

"I'll make it snappy," said Reed, yawning in a little room, "where were you last Monday? That was the day when one Giles Cream died."

"I cannot say," said Pidal with a kind of hostile sullenness. "If I did it would not help. I would not know my way about Larchmont, and the old lady and her servants are there all day." He stopped. Nervous, thought Reed, to blurt out such an admission.

"I wouldn't blame you for taking a good look at it," said Jarvis with unction, "with so much bad blood between you and the dead man."

There was silence.

"It might make it more convenient for yourself if you made a statement," said Reed, his notebook on his knee.

Pidal slicked back his black, thickly brilliantined hair, black eyes slewing round from a smooth, olive-skinned face.

"I had nothing to do with this man's death. A month ago I had cause to tell him to keep out of affairs that have nothing to do with him. I told him it wasn't a case of soothing syrup over the TV in my country, it was guns and he risked injury."

"Who do you represent?"

"A group of people who want no interference from foreigners. In fact we want nothing from you." Pidal's eyes had the fanatic glow in them.

"You tried to draw a gun on us, you know," said Jarvis.

"Anybody can say 'police' and you said it in Spanish, and this alarmed me. In my country I am a lawyer and I think if I am guilty of anything it is carrying a gun without a licence."

"I don't think we are in the mood to be ruthless," said Reed, "providing you surrender your passport and check in here tomorrow at nine."

He registered quick suspicion. Reed gave a little sigh. It was difficult to explain to many foreigners that you did not particularly want to persecute people. He took the yellow covered passport that Pidal produced, briefly checked it and stowed it away. "Okay, señor, you can go."

"This is a trap," said Pidal, "I shall not leave."

Wearily Reed got out his small memo pad and wrote:

'Mr Pidal is entitled to leave this police station. Signed Robert Reed, Sergeant'. He handed it to Pidal who read it.

"I am sure this will be a comfort if placed in my coffin," said the South American.

Jarvis put his head outside the door and called the six feet four desk sergeant, a man who had once been on the Olympic squad as a heavy-weight wrestler.

"Eject this man."

"Beg pardon?" The huge weather-reddened face creased in astonishment.

"Run the bugger on to the pavement and leave him there."

"I'll be damned!" But the desk sergeant gathered up Pidal in his arms. He started to kick, but one big hand dug into his solar plexus. Reed and Jarvis followed them out. Pidal, somehow managing to express outraged dignity by means of his back and thick neck, scuttled away into the late night crowd.

"Might as well get back to the office and dope out a report," suggested Reed as the senior man. He was not due on tomorrow until late afternoon, there was whisky in his drawer and he was experiencing one of his periodic reluctances to go home. And, knowing how Jarvis so relished his late supper money, late duty money, early breakfast money and transport home allowance, it was in a way a kindly thought. His lugubrious colleague welcomed the gesture. Reed's office was deserted, as were most except those dealing with traffic, and the two men seated themselves on the old chairs. As a formality Reed took up a phone and reported 'in' for both of them.

"That's odd." He replaced the handset. "There have been two calls for you from a fellow named Flitch. Isn't he the musician bloke?"

"Yes." Jarvis dragged out his book. "Let's see, here's the number. Might as well: it'll look good in the report." He dialled on the outside line, got through and talked while Reed listened with increasing perturbation. It did not take long.

He was forced to wait while Jarvis with customary stolidity arranged his thoughts, a process which had once been described as similar to the action of a very old, purblind lady setting up a rickety tea set. To show his agitation he extracted a eucalyptus gum—one of his rare luxuries—from his pocket and sucked it. "A rum go," he said, prising its stickiness from his dentures with his tongue. "That fellow, the long-haired fiddler or whatever he is, says that Mrs Hedi Ching has gone."

"Gone where?"

"Her maid does not know. She said she would have a light supper at home when she returned at seven. Flitch was phoning her all evening. I've told him to get over here pronto. I'd better go down to reception."

He lingered at the door. "I don't suppose they can blame us."

"No." Reed lied to reassure him, and when the door closed poured a good measure of Scotch into his old tooth glass which he remembered to wash perhaps once in six months. For himself he had little doubt that if scapegoats were needed he and Jarvis would be the selected ones. He got through to Quant's office and found a deputy, one Chief Inspector Croucher, occupying the desk. No, Quant and the D.C. had taken off for Devizes. He should have known, the Sergeant realised! Whoever found over twenty million pounds worth of loot, seizable by the Crown was on to a good thing for life. The D.C.'s avidity for the Governorship of a Pacific island was more common knowledge than he thought.

Croucher listened to the news and spoke as if wounded. Yes, they could bring Mr Flitch up to his office. Meantime he would get the local Division to send round a couple of men immediately to Mrs Ching's house.

When the lift door opened in thirty minutes' time Reed got in and jerked his thumb at the ceiling. "Quant's room with Croucher in charge. Evening, Mr Flitch."

The American was dressed with the rather elegant casualness for which his countrymen had a flair. It seemed to Reed that he was much better dressed than the night upon which he had seen him at Larchmont. To the Sergeant's eye, trained to observe small details almost automatically, he had shaved carefully that evening and had a haircut that day. He smelled of unobtrusive perfume for men and his nails had been manicured at some not too recent occasion.

Chief Inspector Croucher was a rubicund man for police standards who affected a homely manner, a Yorkshire accent and a pipe. Reed made the introductions.

"Sit yourself down," invited Croucher. "Now why would you be seeking Mrs Ching, sir?"

"I am very much attracted to her," said Flitch. "She is a most fascinating woman."

"Is it not a bit early to move in?"

Flitch gave his rare, lopsided smile. "Giles told me a lot about the lady. To an extent I was his confidant. With Mrs Ching, well she was a lady with whom it might be unwise to let grass grow under your feet. To be more serious she is capable at a moment's notice to take off to some grim South American banana republic."

"But, and do not be offended, she might be a lady used to expensive places."

"I got fifteen hundred pounds today on the strength of my musical."

"So you saw the Creams today, a nice family I believe."

Flitch's smile had vanished. "Ambrose holds the money side there. I am getting my expenses—on a rather cheap scale—and there will be no more until the advance bookings come in. No, I saw Herr Grädde. He's becoming one of the shareholders in their business: a wealthy man with confidence in my work. He advanced the money, at a nominal three per cent," he sounded a trifle rueful, "against my interest in the show. But, well, Sergeant Jarvis has seen my hotel room. It is definitely not what I've been sweating blood for."

The telephone rang. Croucher listened for ten minutes and slammed down the handset. "She is still out. At the hire-car place the dispatcher thinks she evidently spent the day at Kew Gardens. She got there around eleven and dismissed the driver who is her usual one. Oh, it'll probably turn out to be nothing. But thank you for your public spirit"—only Croucher really could get away with such cosy remarks thought Reed. "Sergeant Jarvis will take you down and see you are driven home."

He looked at Reed after the door closed. "One thing," he said, "she only had three pounds with her. She has this maid who lives in—another comes in daily. I must see the local chap gets a commendation, for he wheedled out of her that she always peeped into the mistress's handbag before she went out. This morning she carried only three one pound notes and a little silver. She was cavalier about money. You know, 'to the manner born'!"

"She has a country estate, Little Ellings, near Chichester," said the Sergeant.

Croucher made a note and nodded in dismissal. Reed collected Jarvis, took a cup of coffee at a stall and then shared a taxi.

By the time when Read got in to his office at 1 p.m. next afternoon nothing had been heard of Mrs Ching. She had not appeared at her country home and at her elegant little town house the maid was having hysterics. The D.C. and Superintendent Quant had hired scooping devices to disturb the green-slimed depths of the Kennet-Avon Canal and most of the population of that part of Wiltshire had gathered on the towpath, their jaws moving rhythmically and their faces impassive, like those of the grazing brown cows who nibbled placidly at the rich vegetation. The Sergeant was informed that no less than seventeen treasury officials and an armoured car were standing by to foreclose on the loot.

Left in charge of the less rewarding end of the business, Chief Inspector Croucher's Yorkshire pudding blandness was fast giving way to tartare sauce acerbity. When Reed reported to his office, Croucher, who disliked snatching a sandwich lunch, was alternately gobbling at some provided by the canteen and saying scathing things down the telephone.

"The bitch has vanished into thin air," he observed to Reed without bothering about a greeting. "Even Houdini couldn't totally disappear on three quid. She went into the gardens. It was a quiet morning and an old chap brushing leaves inside the Lion Gate is a woman watcher : he identified a photograph at ten this morning. He said she looked quite normal, 'relaxed' was his word for it. She wore a caramel coloured suit, which checks out with the maid's statement, and carried one of those outsize handbags which was her habit. Nobody saw her leave. We have been through her private telephone list—as long as your arm—and rung each name with no result. Nobody has seen her for the past thirty-six hours. Her last appearance was the night before last when she attended an embassy party"—Croucher visibly sweated. "I sent round one of the old Etonians, very humble, and the cloak-room attaché, or whatever he calls himself, deigned to say that Mrs Ching had been madly gay as ever. Any ideas?"

Reed said : "She might be holed up with a boy-friend. Flitch thought she was a creature of impulse. . . . Yet with her lover still in the morgue she might crave male company, but one doubts an overnight stop. And Kew Gardens, a favourite rendezvous made by blackmailers ! It stinks a bit. I suppose . . . ?"

"According to the report she had never met old Mrs

Cream, therefore she had never been in the house, though of course she might have met Giles during the day—there are two unaccounted hours in our list of his movements, not necessarily significant—and he might have taken her into the house in the afternoon when they were asleep or gawping at TV. On Monday, according to the maid, she said she was doing the rounds of the art shops. A woman of parts, a very sharp collector of late seventeenth-century stuff so it transpires. I've got six fellows sweating round the art circuit, but it covers the devil of an area these days."

"She'd head towards London, I guess," said Sergeant Reed.

"They always do. It's the thrillers that teach them that idiotic thing."

Reed knew that if a private person or persons were after you, London was the best bet: not so if the police were involved, for the London police net was pretty infallible and a moderately sized tourist resort was by far your better bet.

"Trouble is," said Croucher, "that it takes time, and if the press get hold of it, on top of the Cream business, there'll be a gale of adverse criticism, a gale!" His eyes always looked genial at casual glance, but their real coldness was apparent now. "I'll give you a roving commission to do what you can. You can have Sergeant Jarvis to assist."

"Any leads?"

"Any I have are being covered: in any case I do not want to clutter up your thinking."

A capable man, thought Reed as he went down in the lift. They came all shapes and sizes, but Croucher was being groomed to replace Quant when the Super retired. The Sergeant gave a very small sigh and for a moment felt quite old and dyspeptic. It took him half an hour to find 'Crying' Jarvis because that worthy had been so engrossed in filling out his previous day's expenses after finishing his streaky-bacon-and-eggs that he missed his bus. A lesser man might have taken a taxi to the nearest tube station, not so Jarvis who stood glumly watching the traffic beside the 'Stop' sign until the now hourly service provided another.

"A roving assignment," said Reed, "let's get out of here."

Reed had stoked up a little after an early lunch of stewed kidneys which he abominated but which his wife insisted were good for him, so he resignedly acquiesced in Jarvis's choice of a small, basement coffee shop. The provender was so unpleasant that one could always find an unoccupied alcove and sink into the smelly cushions of the divan type seats. They ordered coffee and Jarvis, making a note, a Bath bun. "Pick one with plenty of sugar," he asked the old waitress who sniffed. 'Afternoon refreshment in connection with roving assignment, 8/9d' would in due course appear on his expense docket.

Presently, sipping the murky fluid which had no connection with Java or even Nestlé, Reed said: "We might as well play a long-shot. She's a fast thinking girl with a devious mind."

Jarvis looked blank, psychology was not his strong suit.

"So," continued Reed, "she won't go to friends: she has only three quid, unless she had a secret hoard stashed away somewhere, but that's harder than it sounds. Where do you put it? Of course she might have, say, a post office account somewhere, far-seeing people do, perhaps thirty quid or so. You just might want it, or you can draw on it when you don't want your wife to know you are spending a bit of money on a girl. Again, women used to sew emergency money in their stays, but nowadays. . . I still think woman have lost more than they gained by these modern clothes."

Jarvis ate his Bath bun while he thought. The waitress had done him proud in the thickness of the sugar glazing but the Sergeant, not a fussy man, admitted to himself that it was probably three days since it left the oven. "That seems all right," he said, brushing the crumbs off his shirt front.

"All I can think of is an old friend, ex girl-friend or,

according to reports, more probably a bygone lover. A 'dulling, save muh!' sort of appeal. But where do we get the starters, somebody who knew La Ching years back?"

Jarvis was good on facts, a regular Gradgrind. After cogitating, he said, "I know an old biddy who is a retired gossip—you know, newspapers and mags. Goes back to the twenties when there were the plain blackmailing weeklies, if you remember reading of it."

Reed did. The highest known sum paid for *not* inserting an article was around twenty-five thousand pounds at today's values.

"In the thirties she joined quite legitimate daily papers as an assistant to the columnist. She used to give us quite a bit of info on quid pro quo terms. Inspector Lydd used to tip her certain interesting pars. and she gave him anything she sniffed out in return. They both retired ten years ago. Lydd's a friend of my family, and I met her once or twice at his house."

Somehow Reed had never envisaged the gloomy Sergeant as having family, except his wife and children. "It's worth a try," he said.

"I'll phone, to see that she's in. She's got a nice, warm little bit of property out Finchley way. If she knows anything we might go to see her, you get more out of people like her if you see 'em personally."

Reed insisted it was on him and saw his colleague's face get the nearest to smiling of which it was possible. Jarvis went into the nearest phone box and nodded as he emerged. "She knew Mrs Ching when she was a Miss Angel, a year or so before she retired. She was a potential swimming champion but liked late nights a bit too much. The Gossip sounded full of meat. How shall we go?"

"To tell the truth I feel a bit pooped, not enough sleep."

"We're none of us getting younger," agreed Jarvis.

"So what about dozing in a bus—you can put in for the taxi."

Thus, on the upper deck, they lumbered across London. Reed's chin fell forward on to his shirt front as he achieved the state, common to travellers on long distance buses or trains, wherein three-quarters of the brain sleeps, the remaining quarter registering the noises, change of speed and stops, even managing to signal to the rest that the destination is coming close.

Still half asleep Reed eventually stumbled down the steps behind Jarvis who had spent the journey in calculating how much a Jehu would have charged him by the longest possible route. The Gossip, in his sleepy condition Reed missed the surname, was a comfortable lady clad in a generously cut frock to match her figure and a blue rinse. She wore the octagonal spectacles which the trade describe as fascinating but which in practice add a terrifying dimension to otherwise nice women. She had already brewed excellent coffee and Jarvis's eyes glistened at the rich chocolate cake pre-cut into generous slices. Reed's heart, or more accurately his stomach, dropped, but the Gossip was beaming at him. "I've heard of you, Mr Reed, and perhaps you'd like a Drop of Something. I have whisky, gin or some extra special black rum."

"A little rum to go with the coffee, ma'am."

Inwardly Jarvis cursed him for wasting time while the Gossip disappeared to fetch an ancient looking bottle.

"Sip it separate, my dear," she said, filling a small glass, "it's a sin to put it with anything."

Jarvis was at last at liberty to dive into the chocolate cake, with the Gossip at his heels in terms of ingoings. After twenty minutes, they sat back in their chairs with a second cup of coffee and Reed with another rum. He congratulated his hostess on its quality.

"About Mrs Hedi Ching," he said reluctantly for the room was comfortable, and she did not look the kind of lady who would object to a man taking a nap.

"In the business I was in," she said, wiping her mouth,

"you get to pick the likely colts and fillies, the ones that you can get the public interested in. They've got to project something. I knew the Ching woman when she was a Miss Angel. Came of a cadet branch of a west-country, land-owning family. Only child, ineffectual parents, father found some sinecure by the Family. Oh, my memory is not that good, but I've got every notebook I ever used filed and indexed. It used to be my stock-in-trade and I could cook up a story where the others couldn't. Well worth the hour a day I used to spend indexing. Now they are amusing for me to browse through. Hedi was a born athlete—table-tennis champion, sprint runner and perhaps best of all a two hundred metres swimmer. We—Fleet Street I mean—built her up as a model of young England. Actually she was a hellion. She never liked training so by nineteen her swimming hopes had receded. It was before drugs became the thing, but she drank pretty solidly for that age. She came up to London to stay with a wealthy, titled old aunt who was too absorbed in her work for doggies to care much what the wench did. The old lady probably gave her a dress allowance and she used to do modelling : there was a nice story once when she modelled swim-suits and they threatened to take away her amateur status! She eventually married an oil millionaire—for two years, after which she had graduated from our gay English rose to the Dashing Young Matron stable. Next . . ."

"Just a minute, my dear," said Reed, "what we are after is finding an old, faithful friend, either sex although I suspect the odds would be on a male. We want somebody she hasn't seen much of for some time, somebody she could ask for help."

The Gossip, Reed noticed, had a shorthand-covered paper on her lap. Her shrewd eyes narrowed. "Can I smell a juicy story? The old war mare hears distant strumpets and a nice big cheque."

It was inevitable, Reed knew. Once the ink was in their

veins there it remained. Not that the money counted so much as the thrill of the chase. He said: "The strumpet in question is distant in that she may, repeat may, have disappeared. At the moment any mention of that would probably mean a suit for holding up to ridicule. If your information leads to anything, I promise you either Jarvis or I will tip you off—under the rose—over the phone."

A substantial arm snaked out and opened a drawer in a small writing desk. "Here is my card, Mr Reed, and for God's sake sew it in your wallet."

Reed stowed it away while she read her notes. Eventually she said: "She was engaged four times, once to a baronet, but she changed her dance partners as often as her stockings. Girl friends? My notes indicate that she had none. A man's woman is our Hedi and why not, pray? I have a note of an old faithful, her first fiancé: it lasted three months, but later there is a quote, 'I always creep back to Hubert for comfort and solace'. She always played along, did Hedi. I remember her saying it at the press conference, camping like hell. Beautiful eyes she has, damned if I can recall her face. Old faithful was named Hubert Mutlar."

"Good God."

"Prominent Victorian family gone to seed. Now I once interviewed him for a 'when we are married' par. Handsome in a 'who's for tennis?' way. He'd tried engineering, then the law, but not finished. One of those people with nice, shiny, quite impressive works, but somehow a weak mainspring. I got the impression, from experience, that he got perhaps eight hundred a year nett from the remains of the family fortunes. He was a private book dealer. No shop or anything like that. There are quite a few who make a good living out of that game. Sometimes they even buy from one bookshop and sell at a handsome profit at another. The reason is perhaps that they do not have administrational cares and can concentrate on one thing at a time. You have to be good, and I doubt he was that. He lived in chambers in an old block off Fleet Street, pulled down now to make way for a glass menagerie. That's the only lead I have. Wait a minute." She helped Reed to another rum, offered Jarvis the last of the chocolate cake and coffee which, after a little polite coyness, he accepted. The fact that his cadged snacks and absences meant that the Sergeant often had neither the appetite nor the opportunity to dine at home was a source of acrimony between him and Mrs Jarvis, the Sergeant wishing to deduct a little something from the house-keeping and the lady saying it really made no difference. He was thinking glumly of this while his hostess went and searched the phone book.

"The sort of man who has to live in London," she said. "Here he be, mouse-holed up in Aberdeen Park, a block of flats by the name of Hornby Heights."

She tried three times before shrugging and hanging up. "Not a peep out of 'em. Our friend Hubert is probably still carrying the torch : most housewives are at home at this hour. Hey, ho." She scribbled and gave the slip of paper to Jarvis. "It's over to you, so here is the address. Don't forget to phone me if something breaks."

Reed had slyly helped himself to a slug of rum.

There was a taxi rank nearby. Without having to think of it, Jarvis merely said, "Aberdeen Park." He consulted his pocket map-book and presently gave a street address two blocks away from Hornby Heights, which was where Mr Mutlar lived. It was 5.15 when they alighted and the pubs were open. Jarvis groaned when he saw this, although brightening a bit as Reed paid and waved away the offer of "halves".

"You put it on yours, old man, and come and have a wet. My brains are dry."

In the yet deserted saloon, Jarvis had a grapefruit and Reed a rum, not a patch on the stuff he had been drinking, but rum nevertheless. While drinking rum it was the only time he ever understood how the troops had endured the 1914–18 War. There should have been a monument erected to the stuff.

"Damned if I know what we can do," said Jarvis mournfully. "If she's there, all they'll do is not to answer the door or the phone."

It took a surprising nerve to do that, mused Reed, to sit in a silent flat while the doorbell or the phone rang and rang. Your nerves started to jump at each peal. He judged that Hedi Ching had her nerves under control. He went over and got a beer chaser. "Better have a look at the place," he said after he had finished, feeling the bitterness flush away the sugar from his mouth.

Hornby Heights was a towering place. There was a doorman. Antique books must be paying off! Hubert Mutlar was in 821. Reed looked casually upwards, counting. The floor looked as though it might comprise the smaller, two-room apartments. There was a telephone box nearby. "Wait for me," he said and entered. He got through to Hornby Heights and asked for the manager. A rather harassed voice answered.

Reed had a certain talent for mimicry and now he adopted stage Mayfair, not bothering to disguise the pitch of his voice as few people can swear to that as the result of a telephone conversation.

"Hornby Heights? The manager? Ai was passing 821. Have you got thet—821? There was a strong smell of guess. What's that? I said 'guess', a guess-stove or a guess-fur"—for one awful moment the remote contingency occurred to him that it might be all electric—"as I said there is a ver' strong smell of guess indeed. My name? My waif and ai have no desire to be mixed up in anything." He put the handset down.

Beckoning Jarvis he crossed the road rapidly, nodded to

the porter, and with Jarvis entered a waiting automatic lift. He dialled eight.

The carpeted corridor was deserted, all the wifies back home with most of the kiddies, and the hubbies still preparing to come home.

"What gives?" asked Jarvis.

"Better you be ignorant!"

They strolled slowly the length of the corridor and turned to come back. 821 was further along, almost opposite the lift. At that moment the lift door opened and the porter and a small wizened man came smartly out of it. They then rang the bell of 821 while Reed bent and undid and did up his shoe-lace. After a couple of minutes there was no reply and the hall porter started beating with his fists. You can't tie up laces indefinitely so Reed and Jarvis stood outside 834 as though waiting for the door to answer. It was just as well, for the manager gave a swift glance round before producing the pass key. It is not an instrument which well-bred managements like to advertise and many tenants remain for their lives in happy ignorance. He inserted it and opened the door, and as he and the hall porter entered, Reed followed by Jarvis were on their heels.

"What the hell . . ." said the porter.

"Scotland Yard." Reed brandished his warrant. "We were passing. Is something wrong?"

A door opened and a tall thin man, hair beginning to recede over a conventionally handsome face, very English in conformation, came out of the end room. It was as he thought, summed up Reed, a living-cum-dining room, bedroom, kitchen and bathroom set-up.

"What the devil is this?" asked the thin man, but there was an undertone of nervousness behind the bluster.

"Gas, Mr Mutlar, sir, somebody smelled gas and there was no answer to the bell and the knocks so . . ."

"So you forced your way in," said Mutlar, gathering confidence.

"It is my duty to protect our guests' interests I'm sure," said the manager, doggedly. "I was told there was a smell of gas."

Reed had meanwhile edged behind Mutlar who was standing slightly sideways to address the manager. He tried the handle of the bedroom door and pressed. It was locked. Mutlar had moved past him towards the front door, warming up to his onslaught on the manager. The Sergeant bent and looked into the keyhole. The key was in the other side.

"Beg pardon, sir," he said, "but the bedroom's locked from the inside."

"Who might you be?" Mutlar swung round.

"A police officer, sir, who was passing and wondered if he could be of assistance."

"Well you can't. And as for you," he addressed the red-faced manager, "perhaps you'll leave as well."

"There was this report about gas, Mr Mutlar," said the manager, veteran of countless battles with the tenants. "It would set all our minds at rest if you just stuck your head inside that room and sniffed."

"I am not going to stick my head in rooms and sniff," said Mutlar, very slowly and precisely, swinging round to look at Reed again. Jarvis and the hall porter had retreated outside the front door. "I thought I ordered *you* on."

The Sergeant raised his voice. "I am Sergeant Reed, C.I.D. I am looking for Mrs Ching to have a word with her."

He saw Mutlar's jaw drop to reveal horse teeth. There was the noise of a lock turning and slowly the bedroom door opened inwards.

"God damn you," said Mrs Ching, breathing hard.

After one good inhalation in Mrs Ching's general direction, the manager said how sorry he was to have troubled Mr Mutlar and rapidly departed. Sergeant Jarvis came in and closed the door. There were a few seconds of silence.

"I . . ." began Mutlar.

"You see, darling," said Mrs Ching in her rapid, disturbing contralto, "if these men can just come here, anybody else could. I know them, they came to see me about Giles."

Reed noted that her temper was under control again. "That isn't quite true, madam," he said. " 'Anybody' has not the resources we possess. You should be safe here if you are worried about what I suspect you may be worried about, particularly if we keep a rather obvious eye on you." He noted she was wearing the caramel suit she disappeared in. That would be trying for a woman like her, perhaps, but then he remembered that there was another, safari-type, Hedi Ching built into the glamorous city dweller.

"We had better go sit down." With the calm assumption of one in her own home, Mrs Ching led the way into a very large living-room. Reed, who hated small rooms and preferred one large to three small, evaluated the furniture and concluded that Mr Mutlar, apart from his private means, must be doing fairly well in trade unless he had had a further inheritance.

"Do get some drinks, honey," said Mrs Ching, "my throat is quite dry from sheer terror."

On a book case was a photograph of Mutlar and Mrs Ching, obviously taken about ten years previously. Mutlar had faded appreciably, like a colour print exposed to strong sunlight over that period. He trotted obediently to the small bar.

"Dark rum if you carry it," said Reed.

"Which seems a very good idea if made rather large," said Mrs Ching.

Reed noticed that Mutlar followed her lead. Somehow Jarvis's opinion was not asked for and a large rum was placed upon the coffee table beside his chair.

"Are you afraid of one Pidal, ma'am." Reed came straight to the point.

Her diamond-shaped, greenish eyes opened momentarily, but she said without hesitation. "That is true."

"I suppose you met him at Kew Gardens and that he demanded money."

"That is so. He gave me twenty-four hours to get it."

"As far as I can make it out, you and the late Giles Cream were involved in political activity in South America. Pidal, who Mr Jarvis and me arrested last night by the way, is a self-confessed revolutionary."

"You have him in prison?" She showed her white teeth.

"We took his gun and his passport. He reported to the local station this morning like a good boy. I have no doubt that on the basis of your statement, the Home Office will issue an order for deportation. I do hope you may see your way clear to being frank with us, Mrs Ching: an innocent person never has anything to fear from us." The last remark was not quite true, thought the Sergeant, but true enough.

"I think you had better tell them what you told me, my dearest," said besotted Mutlar, looming over the back of her chair. Reed hoped he got some suitable reward in the right place, which he thought might be bed.

"I have, perhaps it should be had,"—just to keep her hand in, perhaps, Hedi Ching half turned and, tilting her head, smiled up at Mutlar—"various political ambitions regarding a certain South American state. If you only knew the corruption and poverty, Sergeant."

"I do not want to."

"That's the trouble with people," she sounded animated, exuding personal magnetism.

"I have enough trouble with crooks along the Thames without bothering about crooks along the Orinoco. And at the end of the day all I want is a stiff drink." He looked meaningly at his empty glass and Mutlar gathered it up to take to the bar.

"Giles, who loathed injustice, was my partner, as it were, in certain plans to overthrow one particularly corrupt régime. I needed him, his prestige for one thing . . . What will happen now, I do not know. I suppose, nothing."

"Are you telling me that this Pidal is one of the opponents of your scheme?"

"You had better tell them *exactly* what you told me, dear." Mutlar had brought back the rum. His voice was dry, but Reed thought that under his apparent ineffectualness there might exist a degree of high intelligence.

Mrs Ching had coloured deeply. "No, not an opponent by any means. He was with us to the extent of wanting the Americans out and a people's régime in. I don't know how to put it. . . ."

"Allow me," said Mutlar. "I have not explored the ends of the earth, but I have explored the ends of a hell of a lot of books. Pidal is your typical revolutionary who, if successful, ends up by becoming something worse than the man he supplants : that is, he is a real revolutionary. Cream got his attitude out of a romantic imagination. When he did this tour of South America he was so sick of what he saw—the reality, the sordid tombola wheel on which the poor never can buy a winning number—that he blew quite cold. I imagine some other crusade—against selling crippled old horses for meat to feed our Common Market friends for instance—might have proven more attractive as a vehicle for his romanticism. To keep his nose at the revolutionary wheel, Hedi—Mrs Ching—decided there had better be a personification of evil in the form of somebody who threatened them. This was the challenge to which Giles's adolescent romanticism would react : it would keep him hot."

"I wish you would not put it like that," said Hedi Ching, momentarily deflated.

Although besotted, Mutlar had a cold logical style—Reed remembered he had once been apprenticed to the Law and that lawyers generally are the only folk who manage to be logical in their approach to sex. "This chap Pidal," he said, " is a fellow traveller with Hedi, at least to the extent of wishing to expel the damn *yanqui*, lavishing as he does huge sums from the unfortunate American tax-payer, from their soil. If you wish to make an enemy, Sergeant, lend or give 'em money. Pidal agreed to act the heavy villain, to threaten Hedi in Giles's presence thus ensuring his adherence to the conspiracy.

"The point," said Mutlar—curse it, thought the Sergeant, the fellow thought he was addressing a county court over a matter of twopence halfpenny, but the rum was quite good—"is that after fellow travellers have shared your compartment for some distance they want to take a different route. You find you have something quite nasty seated opposite you. Hedi and Pidal used to meet in places like Kew Gardens. Yesterday he saw her at noon and demanded ten thousand pounds . . . or else. Hedi did the wise thing and came here. I deal in old books and spend a lot of time at home."

"I wonder what the 'else' was?" said Reed quietly.

"Pidal," said Mrs Ching, "is not a cheap skate. He is a good lawyer and the ruling clique would welcome him, probably make him deputy director of prosecutions or its equivalent, but he will have none of it. There is a very solid foundation for his anti-yanqui sentiments, which none of you would understand, I'm sure. I am afraid I talked to him indiscreetly : he was such a friend, so wise." For a moment she was in despair.

"Giles had found out who his grandfather was. It was Hans Grädde, father of Sven-Eric." She said it quickly.

"He had to have a paternal grandsire," said Reed, reasonably, peering absent-mindedly at his empty glass. Jarvis seized the opportunity to substitute it for his own full one.

"He was one of the richest men in Europe. Armaments, mostly, supplied to both sides, starting with the Franco-Prussian War and the other big one looming ahead. He was a nut, good looking in that snow-white way, but one out of the bin all right. He would only go out at night, had a castle at a place where it is always night, or almost. He was popular, a good party man, but you never invited him to come while the sun was up. And as mean as they ever were. Wasting soap used to infuriate him: he used to pinch odd bits from other people's bathrooms and have his valet boil them down. His correspondence was on the back of letters received and he was a nuisance about string, used bottles and heating costs. When he was forty-two he married Hezekiah Cream, who was twenty-six. She was staying with him in one of his Swedish places and he married her according to Swedish law. They divorced before the child was born, also in Sweden."

"Mm," said Reed, all attention, "I must say I was puzzled by their pigmentation, quite different from the old grannie's. I saw a picture on her mantelpiece, obviously of the son. He could have played the Big Swede in films."

"It was curious," said Mrs Ching. "Giles made quite a lot of arty films in Sweden . . . You know, where they take everything off and drown themselves in the last reel, very slowly to music and drifting petals. Language does not matter nowadays with dubbing a fine art, but he picked up some Swedish, and, of course, Grädde means milk."

"*Of course,*" said Reed, "We all speak Swedish!"

"Why does one get into these clichés," Hedi scolded herself. "But that triggered it off. Part of the settlement was that she should drop the name, but she has a sly sense of humour and made it Mrs Cream. The cream off the milk, so to speak. He didn't much like it."

"Mrs Cream," said Reed, "bought herself an annuity of thirty quid a week for life and the tail-end of the Larchmont lease, hardly a pay-off for the divorced wife of one of the wealthiest men around."

"In an age of blackmailing, beautiful harpies," said Mrs Ching, "Hezekiah Cream was an honest lady. Besides she is a matter of-fact one. Old Grädde owned about every politician around the Baltic : if he wanted divorce who could oppose him ?"

"Public opinion."

"My dear sir," said Mrs Ching, the London School of Economics coming out on her like a hot flush, "this was before 1914. The peasants counted for nothing. If a reporter called, old Grädde would send down a stable boy with a horse-whip. Sven-Eric, his son, has a batch of sauve P.R.O.s at three thousand per year and expenses to accomplish rather less. But, then, there was the will. Old Grädde, middle-aged (as forty-five was then, married the daughter of an English Duke, produced Sven-Eric, and eventually died aged ninety-four, more or less in the arms of one of the Krupp family. Goering was one of the official mourners. He left one of those screwy wills whereby one half of his fortune was to be distributed among the grandchildren, if living, in 1972."

"Lord," said Reed, upright in his chair.

"Sven-Eric Grädde has one son, and therefore instead of getting the lot, he now gets one-fifth. It is a matter of twenty-seven million pounds."

"These figures make me slightly ill," said Reed, "may I encroach upon your hospitality for another rum, sir? The Creams seem destined to be swaddled in millions from cradle to the grave, only the graves seem a trifle premature. Without buckling to arithmetic, it seems to me that had Giles lived, all the grandchildren would have got roughly four and a half million, but that his death means the surviving heirs get about eight hundred thousand pounds additional. I do not know a better motive for murder. How did Giles ferret this out?"

"He taxed his grandma. She doesn't care, but had not told them as old Grädde exacted a promise of silence about the marriage and, although the old swine died of chagrin when Krupp finally elbowed him out of Hitler's good graces, she is still in awe of him. He must have been really something." Hedi Ching looked wistful and could not help a side glance at Mr Mutlar.

"After that he just had to look up the will in the Swedish records office. He saw Grädde who merely said it was something for the lawyers, or so Giles told me four months ago. Grädde was quite frank : his own heir, who is about thirty now, would probably contest the validity of Hezekiah's marriage to the grandfather. You see, I'm afraid that this sort of situation made Giles boil. He considered that his grandma had been wickedly robbed by the squire, though Hezekiah just does not think so at all. She never set her sights at big game, preferring the small pickings with no great emotional upset. That kind of woman!" Though fair Mrs Ching was a bit contemptuous of a less ambitious sister.

"When did Giles confide this to you?"

"Six months ago. I told him . . . I mean advised him . . . to see Grädde. It's obviously one of those situations where there is a compromise. A good lump sum in Sweden would have been a godsend : I have no doubt they could have realised an immediate sum."

"Upon a tontine?" said Reed. "In what they call obit lending, quite large interest is charged, because, you see, sudden death is a wild factor."

The room seemed suddenly very cold.

"There was enough for all," said Mrs Ching hoarsely.

"There never is . . . for some people. When I was a youngster in my teens, a fiver was a lot of money. Then a tenner was a lot of money. In my middle years two thousand pounds seems a lot of money. God knows where it will end, inflation helping. You get a man bitten with avarice so that it runs in his very blood and he becomes a maniac on the subject."

Sergeant Jarvis was content to leave all this to Reed who liked it. He had been thinking of the implications of the regulation governing the expense of footwear used for special occasions. Surely investigating wealthy actors, actresses and society whores might be deemed an occasion for special, fancy footwear. He had had home several pairs of fancy shoes the property of a dissolute, deceased uncle of his wife, who had filched his clothes while making arrangements for the cremation. He might be able to work a pair in at, say, five pounds ten. They were undeniably almost new, albeit two sizes too small for the Sergeant who had been waiting for his sons to grow into them.

"Very well," said Reed, swigging the remnant of rum. "So Pidal was threatening to make a fuss about this?"

"He seemed to think," said Mrs Ching, "that he had a property worth blackmail . . . a statement to one of the Sunday papers . . . and of course he said he could have acid thrown in my face by one of the comrades."

"I have to ask you professionally if you want to lay a charge, Mrs Ching. I'm stretching things quite a bit even listening to you."

"Perhaps," said Mrs Ching, "I mean I could give you cash. . . ."

"Hedi, don't," said Mutlar.

"You are a stupid bitch," said Reed, in avuncular fashion. "That is worth six months in itself. I'll put it down to grief, premature change of life and general fatheadedness. Tell me, was he blackmailing Grädde, do you think?"

"Grädde," said Mrs Ching, "supplies arms to South America. There he can be very dangerous indeed. I do not think that Pidal would wish to challenge him. For one thing, if Pidal's side is successful, they will need Grädde, or one of his associates. As for myself, I suppose I must drop the whole idea. I certainly do not wish to charge Pidal. He is a lawyer and God knows what he would invent or say."

"Let me see," said Reed, "Herr Grädde was a particular friend of Giles was he not?"

"Giles? Oh, good God, you do not have the slightest

comprehension of him. He regards unimaginative, dull, efficient Swedish industrialists with abhorrence. Regarded I should have said. It was Ambrose, dear Ambrose, the money-man, who was Grädde's pal."

"I suppose there were no quarrels between the Creams regarding money?"

"Quarrels? No. As I understand it Peter was originally the boss, the man with more than a touch of genius. When he died Ambrose was a very competent impresario with an accountancy degree and no discernible generosity—the others were fairly soft touches, as they say. Ambrose knew that the real talent had missed him by a shade and that his function was to stick close to the others on artistic matters. Oh, he knows it theoretically, from painting the scenery to producing grand opera, but he is dull, dull, dull at bottom. He is, of course, quite exceptional at his job because he knows his limitations. The others relied on him. Giles never had to worry about money matters. If he got a letter needing financial scrutiny it was just marked 'over to you' and sent to Ambrose."

"Very well," said Reed, writing on his memo pad. "In two hours' time, there will be a permanent twenty-four hour guard upon you. And, here, is a telephone number that will produce instant response. Shall you remain here?"

"I think I will," said Mrs Ching and Mutlar could not help emitting a low mooing noise; when he had recovered from the confusion this caused him he handsomely refilled the Sergeant's glass.

Reed got up. "Just do not change your mind unexpectedly, Mrs Ching; that is when trouble can start and we would get most annoyed. I do not think you need anticipate violence."

Mutlar telephoned to the local hire-car service.

Reed said, as they were under way, "Can you drop me and then put in the report? I'll pay thirty bob towards the fare. To tell the truth, I'm tired."

143

CHAPTER SEVEN

THERE WAS RATHER a seething as Reed reported for duty next day. The whole adult population of Devizes, reeling with drink, had seen the dredging operations successfully concluded, a stout pigskin suitcase retrieved with its mantle of green slime. Nothing so exciting had happened since 1936 when a local store manager had gotten, single-handed as it were, fourteen of his female counter hands into what, in Devizes, is termed an interesting condition.

At nine o'clock the D.C. had been summoned to Downing Street, excited as a bride, but to his horror the Big Feller had observed that Men like the D.C. were a pillar, indeed a pride, of the old country and what a pity it was he had never interested himself in the trades unions. Nevertheless, he was instantaneously promoted to full Commander, at an additional increment of three hundred and fifty pounds per year. Quant came out better, being now able to write Chief Superintendent of Detectives on his memos. The D.C. had, after being promised the minor decoration such as was usually reserved for ancient charladies in British Embassies and the wealthier pop-singers, gone back home to weather the imprecations of his wife and daughters. Driven out, he had made his way to his room in Victoria Street where he brooded in sullen silence while two workmen furiously hammered away at the task of removing the brass plate cemented into the corridor wall beside the door of his office. ("Always give a man his new rank at once," was a dictum of the Big Feller, part of his cullings of stale sayings from Harvard Business School!).

Somehow, on the strength of the Dockern jewellery, now confiscated by an Order in Council, the country would be able to borrow two hundred million from the Swiss banks to be spent on the importation of dried fish from Ghana in place of New Zealand lamb, such fish, as a tittering young aide had confided to the then D.C., tasting of old horse manure; but the project (a) teaching the trade unionists that the Master meant business; (b) vastly improving our prestige in Africa; (c) training palates for Common Market fare was important.

While the Commander thought dolefully of such matters Quant was enjoying the box seat, there having been a very distinct hint of a life peerage, albeit still a will o' the wispish light over political bogs ahead, needing goatlike leaps from safe tussock to tussock, as a kind of crown to his career.

He was reading a paper from the research department with a view to finishing his paper on Gibraltar on the possible pernicious effect of bullfighting upon English morals. Mithraism, he noted. A splendid thing if the Archbishop, in his fruity voice, could be persuaded to deliver a diatribe against Mithraism! The patronage of popes—Quant hesitated—there were a damned lot of R.C.s particularly in the working class constituencies. Worse was to come. Nuns making a few passes at the bulls, and fully two hundred bullfights to celebrate the canonisation of St Teresa of Avila, the lady who levitated, remembered the Superintendent. It always was so easy when it was a Popish or I.R.A. plot! He scanned further. There was a Canadian bullfighter of note. He sighed when he saw that the *espada's* name was Henry Higgins. You really could not make a Fascist villain of Henry Higgins. The R.S.P.C.A. was, he feared, the only card he held, and then the Spanish would carry on about staghounds and whipping children with electric flex.

He even wondered if Reed's fertile brain could think of

anything. It might be possible momentarily to encourage the fellow's thoughts towards a belated inspectorship, which was by now quite impossible.

Therefore he summoned the Sergeant.

"Congratulations, Mr Quant," said Reed smoothly enough. The Superintendent noticed that the man's nose was more than ordinarily festooned with small, reddish pimples. Rum, diagnosed the teetotal Quant.

"A small problem, Mr Reed," said Quant and outlined it.

Reed twined and untwined his thick fingers. "Gambling, Mr Quant, might be the answer. The Spanish disapprove of gambling. Oh, there's a lottery, but it's hardly a gamble, as you have to be a relative of an official to get any of the higher prizes. On the other hand Gibraltar's full of gambling. If the working class spend their money on bull fights, at thirty bob a ticket at the running rate, they don't have money to gamble with. They know it in this country, which is why they ruined the cinema industry and won't have pay television. Just alert the Gibraltar millionaires to what would happen if you had a couple of bullrings there and they'll make an outcry. I understand most of them are Hindus and don't like cows being maltreated on principle."

Quant sucked the top of his huge old fountain pen. As usual Reed was right in a coarse way. It would need all the delicacy of which he was capable to put it in the style in which it could be delivered, via an under-secretary, to a bored and comatose House of Commons around eleven-thirty one night. Rendering unto Caesar—there might be something suitably sonorous along those lines.

"I'll think about it," he said, shortly and put the sheet to one side; he then took hold of the file marked, tradition-ally, 'in the matter of Giles Cream, deceased'.

"You have seen the transcript of Jarvis's report?"

"I have nothing to add," said Reed, and indeed Jarvis had reported like a gramophone record.

"How did you get in in the first place?" Quant was curious.

"Somebody had smelled gas. Jarvis and I happened to be passing by as the manager was using the pass key. In accordance with general instructions covering accidents and emergencies we went in with him," said Reed solemnly.

Quant had always been far too cautious to use such ruses himself, but he gave an approving nod as he made a note upon his pad marked 'uninvited entries due to emergency or humane considerations'.

"It is one of two things, sir," said Reed. "One that there is a mad, greedy Cream who wants to take all. Or else Herr Grädde does not want to see a great chunk of money go to what he may well regard as byblows."

"I do not think a man like Mr Grädde, Director of the International Bank that he is, and our supporter when events make it necessary for a wee bit more in the borrowing line, could be mad," said Quant primly. "Coming back in the car, the Commander wondered whether old Mrs Cream could be deranged." He flapped a white hand over the desk. "The Commander has got a lot of gossip about her from his club cronies. She used to ride to hounds, and not side-saddle, but with one leg on different sides of the animal. And shoot, alongside the men, partridges, pheasants, deer and grouse : also clay pigeons! An athletic young lady used to blood sports. I was reading a pamphlet in the course of duty which pointed out that killing a harmless bull is one short step to killing harmless men. Very persuasive it was."

"We must realise that she is very aged, sir. All passion long since spent, or perhaps sold in view of her career."

"There was that old fellow in Scotland," mused the Super, "who did in the maid at eighty years of age. Lust was the motive, and, let's face it, we find in our work that greed is an even stronger motive."

"I like Grädde," said Reed stubbornly.

147

It was plain to the old Super that Grädde should be 'looked into' as official phraseology had it. It was no task for a man with a life peerage beckoning him, a man who, if he had not so far precisely walked with kings, had sustained the damp, brief touch of a Prime Minister's palm. Quant had a good idea of the Commissioner's present mortification, though why the man should wish to live abroad was beyond his comprehension. This was a time when he should make some kind of safe decision without worrying his superior. His fountain pen squeaked as he made out a minute. Clearing his throat, he said: "To possibly clear a distinguished foreigner of any imputation of involvement in felony, you and Sergeant Jarvis are authorised to clarify the position of Herr Sven-Eric Grädde in re the possible murder of Mr Giles Cream. That I think covers the issue, does it not?"

"It covers the issue," said Reed. There was a grimness in his voice which made Quant put down his pen.

"We are not entirely our own masters, Mr Reed," he said. "We do not want to offend Important Nations which by some process which I do not fully understand has come to mean any nation not inhabiting the British Isles, but in particular Germany, Sweden, Switzerland and the U.S.A. You are experienced in the kid-glove methods, and so is Sergeant Jarvis. Suborn the servants, wheedle the cook, ply the coachman with strong waters, but do not insult Mr Grädde himself. There must be nothing served up at embassy level."

"That is understood."

Reed found Jarvis wrapping up a pair of fancy looking shoes with an expense docket.

"Had to buy them for this high society work," said Jarvis, without greeting. "Five pounds ten. They can put them in the Disguise Cupboard."

"We might be doing the rounds of crowned—in the monetary sense—heads today, so put them on." Reed looked cruelly at Jarvis' scuffed eleven-size brogues and then at the dapper nine-fitting dress shoes.

"Can't be bothered." Jarvis hastily tied the packet up with neat knots.

"They retrieved the rest of the jewellery at Devizes."

"So I heard," grunted Jarvis, "and I hope an *ex gratia* is coming our way."

"Five hundred apiece for you and me in the final wash up, according to precedent, but don't bank on getting it in under three years by when it will be worth around two hundred."

Jarvis grunted.

"And now we are on the dirty work squad, to be disowned if necessary," continued Reed.

Jarvis shrugged. "I do whatever they like. If they canned me they're up for a three-quarter pension, so sod 'em all. I'll soldier on. Five hundred quid, eh? I might put it in the wife's name, though with her asthma it's odds on she'll predecease yours truly. Perhaps a trust for the kids, but you can't control your own money that way, and suppose one of them dies early?"

"I think we'll see this fellow Flitch first," said Reed.

Jarvis put the packet in his 'out' basket. "He notified a change of address. A classy little one-room apartment off Soho, restaurant service and black glass bathroom."

Reed looked up the number. He thought Flitch sounded apprehensive and noted that the man did not, as might have been expected, make any enquiry concerning Hedi Ching.

He indented for a pool car. Such was the degree of confusion—the Commander's sudden appointment sadly perplexing the administrative hierarchy that there was not the usual 'explain please' (old Gideon was rumoured to have had the fit that his careless eating habits had cast him for, and there was a rumour that Sir John, despite genteel and gentile senility, was to be lured out of his academic post in

Canberra where he had an interest in breeding stud merinos by an improved system of artificial insemination).

Flitch had done himself well. Reed wondered whose advice had been taken, London being notorious for the foulness of its short-term apartments, mostly old houses amateurishly (with the aid of gas rings) transformed into 'studio dwellings'. But Flitch's pad smelled of *poules de luxe*, French bath essence and *vol-au-vent financiére* with decently cooked potatoes. The paintings on the wall were kind, unframed, and done in plastic colours without stretchers or glass. The mirrors, although discreet, were convenient. There were six conservative and comfortable chairs, the bed folding into a couch during the day.

"I'm not satisfied with your statement regarding Mr Grädde," said Reed, for once disdaining a Scotch.

Jarvis emitted a dismal noise, half-way belch, part lamentation of human nature.

One thing about the Yanks, thought Reed, was that they were so indoctrinated by *Time* and *Newsweek* concerning police brutality that they ran scared from the start unless they were hardened professionals.

"I am willing to repay part of the money," said Flitch stupidly. He was a conductor, remembered Reed, not quite as moronic as tenors but well on the way towards it.

"You put a hard word on the Herr?"

"I insisted on a memo of agreement, just a loan, nothing of the extortion business," stammered Flitch. "I wondered that he had the nerve to complain. He'll get his effing money."

So Flitch had not telephoned Grädde, thought Reed, then remembered that the Swede slept during the morning.

"I think you are being cunning, Mr Flitch, but then artists are notoriously above the moralities. Whether you will ever repay Mr Grädde is something I will not know. He did not complain. I *know* that you know about the inheritance from the Grädde estate. I think you were going to 'borrow' a little from Mrs Ching : your love story was rather sudden. I suppose there was some documentary evidence among the papers he left with you and which you read. Now listen to me very carefully! I have no doubt that you can produce documentary evidence that the money was a loan. In case you feel creative about it, I must tell you that standover men, blackmailers or what-have-you, always use this technique, and judges smirk about it when instructing the jury to ignore the whole alibi. In this case the police have no intention of laying a charge. Under our law the initiative would have to come from Herr Grädde. It is therefore to your advantage to blacken his reputation."

"You are not arresting me?"

"My dear sir you are not a Chicago negro. We have to have written forms!"

"Or a Hindu!"

Flitch was perking up, a good sign during interrogation, and Reed smiled. "Not Jamaican either!"

"Have you tried the Hindu herbal remedies, sir?" smirked Jarvis. "They do cause the rheumatics to fade away, and I suppose your conducting and waving your arms about continually must give you the screws all right as well as making you weak in the nut."

"Conductors are non-arthritics, the cause being the healthy exercise," said Flitch.

"Have you thought of death, Mr Flitch?" asked Jarvis.

"Death?"

"You are messing around with it, sir! A lot of money is involved . . ." Jarvis gave his groan and Flitch turned white.

"I do not see why anybody should murder me. I am an American citizen."

"I dare say that your status does confer some kind of immunity except in the East, sir," said Reed, "but you might encounter some ignoramus who did not enquire of your passport first."

"You're a bit wrong about my finding it among Giles's papers," said Flitch, sullenly, "he told me about it. Oh, there was a bundle of photostats among the papers, but I knew that Grädde was his father's half-brother. Giles was mad about it: his parents were pretty poor, you know, and spent the Depression sweating away with the cheaper brand of concert parties."

"Would he have skinned Grädde's estate?"

"He seemed to think the family should get every penny it was entitled to. What burned him was that Sven-Eric had never revealed the matter, nor given the old lady a farthing. Giles thought that Sven-Eric's 'friendship' was merely a method of spying on the family."

"What did the others think?"

"They did not know." Flitch massaged his jaw and a very sharp horse-trading ancestry peeped out of his blue-grey eyes.

"But the old lady . . . she knew that Giles knew?"

"An odd-ball that. Her position, according to Giles, was that she was satisfied at having twenty-thousand pounds invested as an annuity from old Grädde in lieu of damages. I doubt whether a woman could stand the fellow long-term: neither could she afford to get in his way. Giles said there were odd stories concerning business rivals who went out for a quiet sleigh ride and were never seen again. It was a different age, Sergeant. In the U.S. you could get a bullet in you over an oil lease, my own grandfather was found chewed by the 'gators during the Florida land boom. And by the standards of her time it was a fairish whack, y' know. That she invested it in fixed income is only saying she is another person hoaxed by *rentes* and your equivalent, consols. She did not want to talk about her marriage to Grädde. Giles thought it had not been pleasant and she just cut it out of her mind, a habit she has. As far as he was concerned, he did not mention it to the others."

"Odd," said Reed.

"It is an odd relationship, whatever it was once," said Flitch thoughtfully. "It is purely on an artistic level and as far as Ambrose is concerned, upon a money one. It is not that they dislike each other, but that they no longer think of each other as persons."

"Then they might kill each other," said Reed, sharply. "It is always when people cease to have humanity in the eyes of a murderer that he will destroy them. Oh, there are exceptions, but people rarely kill those they like."

Flitch looked a trifle green.

"We'll keep an eye on you." Reed scribbled, and handed over the slip of paper. "This number brings you instant police service complete with sirens and very tough gentlemen. Just one thing, would Peter Cream have known?"

"I asked Giles that. Peter was an immensely shrewd cookie from all accounts. I mean, one is always interested whether there is any money hanging around unclaimed in the family. But there again, Peter had the secrecy common to them all. Giles replied that he thought so, that there was something on Peter's mind in those last few weeks."

"What exactly transpired between you and Grädde?" said Reed.

"He doesn't get up before noon. At that it is better than his father who kept the shutters clamped throughout the day, or so Giles said. I got into see him around 2 p.m., and said I knew the loss must be the greater for him because of the blood relationship. A cold fish. He invited me to have a coffee. There is a whey-faced secretary who obviously is very conscious of who provides bread, butter and jam. I told him that Ambrose was as tight as a clam as far as advance money is concerned, and, hell, this thing is a watertight success, everybody says so. Grädde asked how much, so I said fifteen hundred of your pounds. I should have made it more, but I was a little uncertain. At a nominal straight interest to cover the book-keeping, I told him. He drew up a note of hand and signed a cheque then and there. The conversation was strictly sterile. Oh, he was quite pleasant in a chromium-sheeted way."

"Then you thought of Mrs Ching?"

"I am attracted to her, Sergeant. I guess I never met a woman like that. I mean, hacking around conservatoriums you get determined, biggish-assed ladies training their full contraltos or devoted to the cause of being among the violins. And after work it always seemed I was too tired, didn't have enough money or was in the army. This week I smelled money around: from what Giles said the little woman was interested in the do-ray-mi as a means, not as an end. I guessed she knew more than I did. I thought that a beautiful partnership might evolve. Tell me, is this off the record?"

"You'll have to rely on my word for it. In fact I doubt anything you have told us is evidence."

"Well, I never met anybody quite like Giles, or the whole family come to that. Back home it's mostly money, like have you got a hundred thousand dollar home which means you are a big executive or an actor? Marxism is a dirty word apart from in the universities where they don't understand what they are saying. But the Creams are Marxists; they have got to have money: it passes their comprehension why people should not have money. I do not know whether, apart from working on stage or film, they know what it is to be poor and eat hamburger meat twice a day. Economic royalists: good God, this is the century of the economic Marxist!"

"I like money," said Jarvis, "everybody does."

"Now we're talking. I came to accept their point of view. I can write pretty good music. Why shouldn't I have money? The Grädde family are the old fashioned Merchants of Death, with their great factories turning the stuff out, financing Hitler and awarding prizes to novelists no one ever heard of. I tell you, if I could have seen a way of carving a quarter of a million bucks off Grädde, I'd have done so. But *you* have nothing on me."

"I am afraid, Mr Flitch, that you benefited from Mr Giles Cream's demise." Reed had his little notebook in one hand.

"Benefited? His will?"

"I know nothing of his will, but upon his death his knowledge descended to you and Mrs Ching, a piece of knowledge as concrete as any treasure. I dare say the Gräddes might have thought two million dollars cheap at the price. So you, or Mrs Ching, or both, with or without accomplices, might have killed Giles to acquire the property."

"I never thought of that." Flitch slumped back in his chair, mouth slack.

"I will tell you something, Mr Flitch, that we have our barristers, very cultivated men who do nothing but court work. There are also immensely shrewd clerks attached to them. In their oily, courteous voices they make it sound pretty deadly in court. The jury don't look at you when they come in. 'Put up Mr Flitch' is the call. The old gent on the bench says 'life'. I'd get yourself a smart solicitor, your Embassy will tell you of a good one. I can't make deals. But if there is any talking you wish to engage in, get a cab, a solicitor and go to see Superintendent Quant or his deputy. Your solicitor will know the ropes."

"I'm quite innocent."

Reed thanked him and went out with Jarvis. He stood for a good minute staring at his toes.

"I don't like this one bit," he said. "Men with Grädde's pull just spit on you. There was that racing case . . ."*

Junior by eighteen months, Jarvis could allow himself the luxury of melancholy silence.

"I'll put through a call to Mr Quant. There's a pub

* *The Odds on Death* (Gollancz)

opposite. We could have an early snack luncheon on me, Mr Jarvis, on me."

Jarvis got through a tin of tomato juice, while Reed, known in this hostelry as in others got through a Campari mixed with Dutch gin, orange juice, Schweppes ginger ale with a slight dash of tonic water, to the horror of a scholarly young gentleman with hairy warts who had come in to use the lavatory and was nervously drinking a brown ale as a kind of repayment.

Presently Reed took a little pleasure in torturing Quant, who had been seated in a pleasant reverie concerning the House of Lords and wondering how life peers were ranked. Were they poor relations, allowed only to use the serve-yourself dining-room? Not that to be a poor relation in such surroundings dismayed the old Super.

"Ach," he said gloomily. "I'll put a twenty-four hour surveillance on Flitch. It might be handy if it is him. The Yanks are willing to sacrifice a national to intensify their image of fairness, particularly if he has no money."

"I think that I will have an early lunch and go to see old Mrs Cream, who obviously knows more than she has been prepared to divulge."

"I do not have to tell you to handle her with kid gloves. Dogs and old ladies, you know!"

"She drinks."

"Yes, yes, I remember. At her age, the beldame. Perhaps it's a good idea."

"And somebody should see Grädde. It looks beyond casual involvement, International Bank or not."

"It is a rare thorny bed," groaned Quant. "Between two old sweats, old Gideon made a rare mess of it while the Commander was not available. Sir John is flying back from Canberra to help muck out but there is some difficulty in insuring him, though he's the man to see Grädde. They were both at Oxbridge and speak the same language."

156

"I didn't know Sir John knew Swedish." The retired Commissioner had once given Reed a bottle of Australian sweet white wine which was corrupt, and the Sergeant had held a grudge ever since.

"What's that! No, no, the Commander has just rung and Downing Street is on the other line regarding Gibraltar and bullfighting. Do your best!"

"In a mess I expect as usual," said Jarvis enquiringly. In fact he did not care. Reed's offer to pay for lunch had impaled him between roast goose at seventeen and sixpence, which he loathed, and Toad-in-the-Hole* which was five bob and upon which he doted. His economic thoughts thrust him towards the goose, while his gastric juices hauled the other way. He settled for steak *marchand de vin* at thirteen bob.

Reed did not feel hungry. Nowadays he often did not, but forced himself to munch a mushroom omelette, drinking keg bitter while Jarvis gloated over a double portion of chocolate meringue pie and whipped cream.

It was 1.30 when they arrived at Larchmont. When did the old lady go down for her zzz? Neither sergeant could remember, but Miss Birch, who had mayonnaise and tinned salmon round her mouth, said that the old lady was eating *en famille*.

They were all there at the long mahogany table, the remains of a luscious game pie, shattered like a defeated gladiator, on the sideboard, while Mrs Rumming rapidly dissected cheese soufflé from the warming plate.

"Have you eaten?" asked Sally Cream.

"No," said Jarvis swiftly.

Mrs Rumming rapidly pushed forward two extra chairs. Jarvis opined that a little cheese soufflé might be very comfortable; Reed, with the knowledge that they usually put a fortified red wine in it, asked for game pie, realising that

* Foreign readers! These are sausages in fatty batter and best avoided. Ed.

157

the alcohol boiled away during cooking but hoping a bit might have lingered.

As though reading his thoughts, old Mrs Cream said: "Put the port on the table, Rumming, and leave us."

If people would only be sensible and recognise that food was an adjunct to drinking, to be taken in a relaxed atmosphere, the world would be a better place, thought Reed rubbing the crust into the rich jelly. Not that the Creams were terribly relaxed, he noticed.

"Whilst we love to feed you," said Ambrose Cream, pouring coffee, "one supposes that you are not here under the impression it is a restaurant."

"I rarely raise my voice," said old Mrs Cream, "but you are all guests here, including these two police people. I am truly sorry, Mr uh, but they are imperious persons, one is afraid."

"Like grandpapa," said Reed.

"Oh, dear," said the old lady and slopped her port on to the cloth.

"What the hell?" said Dick Cream, moving lithely in his chair.

"We will take it quietly if you please," said Reed.

"I don't know if you ladies and gentlemen have seen the statistics on blood pressure, as it affects the heart and produces curious numbness in the nether regions, but I always caution suspects to remember it, having had sixteen attacks, eight fatal, thrust upon me," Jarvis groaned out his words. "And me having to give suitable evidence to the inquest."

"What is it about?" Mrs Cream finished her soufflé.

"Your grandson, Giles, discovered that old Hans Grädde, father of Sven-Eric, had left half his fortune in a long distance trust for his grandchildren: and that your son by him was born in lawful wedlock. So these lucky young people benefit by millions each." Reed said it quietly.

There was a stillness in the air.

Eyes flicking round, Reed would have sworn they had not known. Jarvis, his face stony, met his glance and gave a little negative shake of his head.

"I do not know what you are talking about." Ambrose Cream said it more as a gambit than a statement, looking at his grandmother. Almost like water suddenly boiling, there was acquisitiveness in the air.

Mrs Cream was unperturbed. "If anybody ever says they will not be bullied, my dears, he is a liar or very foolish. Some people cannot be fought by people lacking their power. Hans Grädde was one of those. I must tell you that . . . I did not have much choice. He set me up in a gloomy Swedish apartment. He never got up during the day. Often he would do nothing but play bezique from 6 a.m. onwards, both of us propped up in bed and the factotum bringing the cheapest sausage and bootleg gin. Horrible stuff. Occasionally he lashed out on a bit of cheap smoked fish. The room smelled of it towards the end."

"You didn't have to do it," said Sally Cream, outraged, "I mean the smoked fish bit."

"It was a very hard year," said Mrs Cream, "the war— when General Smuts was killing 'em—was at an end, and of course there was a panic. You have to have a war somewhere, my dears, otherwise the city gents panic and won't lend money. I do hope the Americans don't stop. . . . We can't afford it, though the Chinese look full of promise."

"Grandmother," said Dick Cream, "after your many sinful years I should hate to have to visit you in Holloway! It would be solitary confinement because the wardresses these days are afraid! What are you up to?"

"Well," she said, "one day he brandished a document at me which he said cost the equivalent of four bob in those days and took me to a register office. He actually went out into the half-light, it being winter. He never had an electric car and got a horse-cab from the local rank. A month later

I'd started your father. As I said Herr Grädde was a masterful man, though I always thought I should have one and he had one of the best brains in Europe : millions of people his ammunition had killed, as he said so proudly. Four months before the baby was due he'd got other papers. Divorce, he said. I was a bit relieved : he'd found a new source of even cheaper smoked fish and the servants were leaving. I just signed 'em and your father was born in Balham Hospital, considered a bit odd then, people having them at home. Hans knew about the child and said when it came he would make provision. Some years later I wrote to the address he gave and he gave me money to buy an annuity of thirty pounds per week. That was the last of it."

"A man who was worth millions," snorted Joan Cream.

"In my time, it was difficult to make a living, particularly a country girl whose family had died out. A slavey? A companion? Fifteen bob a week and live in? Welfare? We had to make our own bed and lie in it ! It was fair enough and there wasn't the income tax snooping at you."

"You never told this to anyone?"

"To nobody. Hans Grädde and I shook hands on it. I must say that you people never saw how Mr Grädde could *look.*"

"The present Grädde is the one that rather interests us," said Reed.

One thing was that with people of this calibre you did not have to press a point too hard. Dick Cream said : "I in fact do know Sven-Eric's only son, the only one of us who does. Is that so?"

"Never saw him from Adam," said Joan Cream, and the rest nodded.

"He's not a bad cabbage," said Dick. "Oh, he's got directorships on a 'yes, dear daddy' principle. But he has a lot of money, no children, his hobbies being large farms and small but nubile actresses. . . ."

"Like his grandpa in one way," said Mrs Cream.

"But my point is that he is not the sort of man to whom a great deal of inheritance means much. He must be worth five millions in his own right. *We* want money to do things with it. He does not. He has his old masters, his young mistresses, and the best stud bulls in Scandinavia upon his model farms. The Grädde covetousness has missed him as far as money is concerned. You'd probably like him. He is as unlike old Sven-Eric as could be except for looks. I suppose we are nordic, come to think of it. Mama was the southern English-rose type, like gran' come to that. There's a difference in the skin texture."

"And what do you propose to do about the inheritance?" asked the Sergeant.

"I'll get the best legal talent forthwith," said Ambrose. "You have papers, Gran?"

"I destroyed them as part of the agreement. You see, dears, I'm afraid this is just a mistake. Mr Grädde was so busy he probably forgot to make the will water-tight."

"A man who partly financed seven major South American wars," said Ambrose, "does not forget things. And you have told us about his queer streak of malice!"

"He had a perverted sense of humour," said the old lady, looking at a picture on the wall. "I must say, in those days, some of the things he did were amusing. He gave a fabulous 'surprise' party once at the Savoy. It cost him eleven thousand pounds in 1910. Oh, his meanness was in his personal life! He invited seventy people, all of whom hated one another. He had employed private detectives for weeks to get it straight. Some of them were society blackmailers and their victims. There was a Duke who had once lived with a stable-boy: he had both along. Then he had Madison Avenue torn up during the night. He was visiting the States at the time and bribed the roads department. The President was due to drive along next morning. . . .

Other things were not so nice, my dears, not so nice at all."

"And so," said Ambrose, his long, smooth doeskin face taut with determination, "the old devil planned all this. I can imagine how he chuckled. It was bound to come out. Lawyers have to advertise as a precaution of their own righteousness. 'All legitimate grandchildren should apply to so-and-so'."

"In my estimation," said the old lady, eyes hard, "Mr Grädde's settlement was final."

"I think what Ambrose is getting at is along two paths," said Joan, wrinkling her forehead. "One is that we have all got one or more children. I cannot sign away the chance of leaving them great wealth. Second, the family business, has suffered a nasty blow from Giles's death—Ambrose and I have done nothing else but consult the accountants—and whatever we do there is probably going to be trouble. Sven-Eric hates trouble, loathes publicity. He'll scuttle back out of much of the business association which is not signed and sealed, and which comprises a hell of a lot. Once the market slips, you can't sell. A banker phoned today humming and hemming about some lousy little twenty thousand overdraft we've had for seven years. We'll clear it tomorrow, ostentatiously, but the gannets will close in, never fear. I would suggest we make a settlement. We need Sven-Eric in this thing."

Reed's eyes warned Jarvis to keep still and listen. A policeman's best friend is a good old family free-for-all.

"I do not think it is honest. A contract should be held in good faith." Mrs Cream looked stubborn.

"I think . . ." Sally Cream had turned on her charm when the door opened.

"Mr Grädde is here," said Miss Birch, smirking.

"One does hope this is no intrusion, and how lucky . . ." Grädde stopped as he saw the sergeants. "Oh, good afternoon, gentlemen. One trusts that this is not intrusion."

"Have some game pie," said Mrs Cream, "I remember that your father used to have a pocket in his coat made of oil cloth — years before plastic, of course — in which he used to stuff things at parties. He always said that game pie carried best apart from ham, but that was considered plebeian in our day. Give Mr Grädde the chair over there, please, Ambrose."

"I have eaten," said Grädde, uneasily seating himself. "Perhaps coffee and brandy."

Reed caught Mrs Cream's eye and was rewarded by a glass.

Ambrose solemnly ate a piece of cheese while the others waited. He swallowed at last.

"It appears that Giles knew about your father's—and our grandfather's—will."

"You knew that of course," said Grädde, sharply.

"We knew nothing of it, even the fact that you are our dearest Uncle Sven-Eric. Or perhaps the wicked uncle."

"Ho, hum," said Grädde. "I assure you not wicked. I took it for granted. Giles—you know his romanticism—said he wished to negotiate solo. I told him, as I tell you, that it would be a matter for the lawyers. I imagine my son will go to the very stuffy, very able firm which represent him and that you will do likewise. It does not matter so terribly. Our family name means 'milk'. My father (a witty man, no?) in his way, used to say that as long as the business, our milch cow, survived, all would be well, and that all folly, excepting gross financial folly, could be underwritten." He coughed. "My son is a little like that, but he knows when to run to the chartered accountants and the lawyers. I have no, repeat no, interest in the matter. I'm sorry that it occurred, but it was before I was born, you know!" He gave a short laugh.

Ambrose's eyes saw Reed finishing the brandy in his glass. "My dear fellows," he said, "I suppose you don't have any interest in a purely domestic discussion."

Reed and Jarvis got to their feet. "A very nice piece of game pie," said Reed.

"A most enjoyable soufflé, I'm sure," said Jarvis. "No, ma'am, don't ring, we'll find our own way out, don't you worry."

There was nobody in the hallway. With a glance at Reed, Jarvis opened the front door and closed it. They then walked back down the corridor to Mrs Cream's sitting-room. There were great bowls of flowers, a peace offering no doubt from the family. Reed, who liked flowers, was disposed to linger.

"I thought we'd take a dekko at the back way," said Jarvis. He opened the door.

"'Allo, 'allo," a stout, elderly man in overalls was squatting on a kitchen chair drinking a quart of stout. The remains of bread and cheese were on a newspaper, and he was scanning the racing page. He introduced himself: "Blachford, the 'andyman wot comes in regular. You'd be police no doubt, sirs, but not the ones that saw me the other day. Not that I could 'elp, never having seen the family except from afar as might be said."

He had the bland stupidity affected by certain members of the Welfare State. Neither sergeant had any doubt that Mr Blachford did all right and that the Inland Revenue and the taxpayer were impotent against him.

"I'm 'aving me lunch," said Blachford, "lunch and the bit of time orf a man is entitled to take to settle his juices before back to the 'ammer, 'ammer on the crool 'ard road, to wit repairing the sashes on two windows. I finish at four."

"I read your statement," said Jarvis, who read everything that came his way. "And you had nothing to contribute."

"A workin' man contributes enough with 'is beer and baccy tax wivout contributing more," chuckled Mr Blachford. "I suppose that wouldn't be your bike? I keep barkin' me shinbones on the bastard. Big old ugly thing, so it is. You'd 'ave to 'ave calves like an elephant to push it along."

"Just a minute." Reed checked his memory for the direction of the kitchen and went there. Mrs Rumming was well into a portion of game pie, the *Daily Mirror* and a pint glass of best bitter.

"You're the copper," she said, "and the glasses are over there; the jug's in the fridge, nice and cool. Not iced, mind you like those 'eathen Australians like it. We 'ave civilisation, I must say."

It was probably the red wine she had used for cooking, thought Reed, as he poured himself a swift pint, for Mrs Rumming was undoubtedly a bit tight, a state not unknown to her profession.

"Where's Miss Birch?"

"She takes 'er delicate liddle tray and bird-like appetite into one of the upstairs rooms. Many a time I find 'er 'acking away at the cold meat in the fridge! Bird like? Oh, yus, but a nostrich!"

"Mr Blachford was asking me about a bike."

"The flipping old bastard. He thought it might be mine. I never been on those things, it being most unladylike. It's my opinion that Blachford got pissed and stole it and couldn't remember it afterwards."

"He doesn't look to me to be much of a bike rider."

"Clumsy as a blind rinoscerus is 'im, breaks more than 'e mends," said Mrs Rumming genially and launched into a fruity-voiced version of 'Glasgow Belongs to Me'.

Reed slipped out, licking froth from his upper lip. He found Jarvis examining the bike while Blachford watched benignly.

"I remember seeing it the night Giles Cream died," said Reed.

"Weren't there two days before which is when I last come 'ere," said Blachford.

"Bell doesn't work, there's no lights or three-speed, tyres oldish," reported Jarvis. "A typical, heavy job turned out around 1934 by a small, back-yard maker. It had some paint put on it, say about thirty-odd years ago, and the chrome isn't bad. I should say it's been kept under shelter. It's had a bit of grease on it very recently : *well* greased, not a nipple missed."

Like most of them, the Sergeant had done his stint on the huge backlog of stolen bicycles.

"Better shut up about this," said Reed to Blachford. "I don't want to disturb the gentry, so I'll just wheel it to the local station."

"Suits me to 'ave it out of the way," said the handyman.

It was a brute beast of a thing, thought Reed as he wheeled it through the backgarden and into the alleyway, catching his shins on the pedal. In the light he saw that its greeny-grey paint was a non-professional job.

"I used to do a bit of road racing," said Jarvis when they reached the road. "The station is about half a mile, if you don't mind walking."

Watching Jarvis' massively twilled-covered seat and legs urging the machine into the landscape, Reed had a vision of the same body, four stone lighter—and with what ambitions?—stoking a racing-bike round Herne Hill twenty years before. But what of himself then? Shooting mostly, not bad at ballroom dancing. Reed belched and plodded along.

CHAPTER EIGHT

Next day the Commander, surfeited with congratulations about his step-up, only his immediate family disagreeing, presided at a ten o'clock conference, rather more highly spiced with superintendents than before, Sergeant Reed banished to a desk within the very shadow of the door, but, in a front seat, was an old constable named Tickle.

It was quite useless to extract anything from the P.C. by way of interrogation. An excellent man, he knew every house and its contents within a limited area of North London and, partly as a duty, was a member of the darts team of The Dog and Duck. At fifteen minutes past nine the previous night, and off duty, he was throwing for a double sixteen in a friendly game of darts and ruminating aloud that the bleeding bike thieves were such a pest that you were only safe if you chained them up. This developed into a discussion about chaining; a morose fish and chip eater at the shove-ha'penny board opined that a sharp tap with a small rubber hammer opened any cheap padlock and wondered why weren't the police a bit sharper at earning the money he, a taxpayer, helped bleeding well provide.

"It's like this, Mr Belper," the P.C. had said, scoring the shot and taking the half pint in a massive hand. "Just before knock-off tonight there was a call about a big, old 1930-ish bike, badly painted grey-green. Urgent it was, fair screaming they were. What about another, Stan?"

The public are notoriously either too eager or too reluctant to aid the course of justice, and it was not until turning-out time that a small man, a retired fishmonger once in a medium way of business, had fastened on to the P.C. as he set off for home. The conversation, minutely detailed by him, was thus.

"Abaht that cycle, P.C., there'd be effing trouble for the pore sod wot owns it?"

"Ar," said Mr Tickle, "not so much trouble, any old 'ow, if he come out with it like a man."

"Well," said the fishmonger after having digested this information. "It might be that it was our Ernie's. We bought it for him cheap in The Cut in 1934 when 'e got 'is scholarship. A reward like and getting 'im to the Grammar School free every day instead of fivepence return. I never did 'old with season tickets. Suppose the boy had died half way through the three munce? Would we get a rebate? The old bleeder in the ticket office said 'no' so I bought the bike."

The P.C. often encountered social problems of this sort. His tongue briefly meddled with the bit of sausage imbedded between two molars before he said, gravely: "You can get a rebate if you turn them in immediate, before the body's cold, like."

"Then we needn't have got the bloody thing and I wouldn't be talkin' about it now. Got his lot at Dunkirk did young Ernie, so you might really say it did do no good at all, includin' the Latin wot they taught him. I can 'ear 'im now. Fucturus Esse, 'e used to say. There we are!"

"Let's hear about the bike, now."

"A pig of a great clumsy bit of cast iron," said the fishmonger.

"I'd 'a chucked it out years ago, but after the News the Old Lady got sentimental abaht it. Used to stroke the seat and cry, kept it in the 'allway under the stag's 'ead my grandpa left, people barkin' their shins and me falling over it when returnin' home of an evening. But now I've had to put the old lady in a institootion, I got to thinkin' abaht it. You 'ave no idea what it feels like to fall over a bike with

168

six pints of keg beer awash in yer bowels. Uncanny is the word the teevee would use. So I put my Thinkin' Cap on." At this point the fishmonger had scratched his bald skull (a point carefully mimed by the P.C., enjoying the crest of a long and diligent career). "The dustmen just laughed in their haughty way after taking a look at it. I gave it to the little kids next door but the farver, a nasty type, said 'e'd kick me where it did most good if I didn't tike it back. But then I thought, wot wiv all the bikes being sent off, why worry? Why not take it to some place and just leave it."

"Against the Law," had said the P.C. "I meantersay you can't have every bastard leaving bikes about the street."

("There's an odd legal point involved," said the Treasury counsel who attended commanders' conferences, and was with difficulty silenced.)

"I've had my own, and I hope last, experience of Treasure Trove," said the Commander at last. "Continue please, P.C."

"He's a Labour man by persuasion, sir, so he took the old bike out one day and left it in the delivery area of a great solicking, posh hotel, just placed it against the wall and scarpered. At three in the morning, in the course of my duty, I took him to identify The Machine." The P.C. capitalised the words as though it were an infernal one. Which in a way it was thought the Commander as he asked, without real hope, could not there be a mistake.

"No, sir," said the P.C. stoutly, " 'e reckons he knows every single fly-blow on the paint."

The point was that the posh hotel was the one in which Herr Grädde had his suite.

"This is very helpful, in the best traditions of the Force," said the Commander in dismissal.

The P.C. bridled, flushed with the knowledge that the following year he might retire with a Sergeant's pension, and all because he liked darts plus a few pints, he ruminated. It was the wages of sin, really, and wouldn't half spite his wife when he told her.

"Well," said the Commander when the door shut, "all paths seem to lead, albeit tenuously, to Herr Grädde."

"A plant?" suggested Quant.

"If I may interpose," said Reed, "Herr Grädde's suite is at the unpopular back part of the hotel. I conclude this is due to his habit of sleeping by day, when the delivery area would be far quieter than the front area on a great thoroughfare. It is my understanding that at any rate heavy deliveries finish by 6 a.m. and dustbins and bottle disposals are also over by then. That would suit Herr Grädde."

"This fishmonger fellow does not look the sort of chap to grease a bike, particularly one kept for years under the deer's head left by his grandfather," said the Commander. "I'm reminded about wheel-barrows. You can guess a country's technicological stage by the incidence of squeak in wheel-barrows. In Sweden it is around one hundred to one against. Swedes are always oiling, greasing and adjusting moving parts. Let's have the map, please."

The outside map of North London came down on its rollers. A technician stood before it with a pointer.

"The route this fishmonger took is quite obvious," said the Commander. "He rode four miles at approximately five in the afternoon a week before Giles Cream died. From the hotel yard to Larchmont offers alternatives. Chalk them up, please."

The tangerine lines showed six ways. "Five and six might be the shot," said the Commander. "Some of you may know the district which is basically a series of triangles, town planning a hundred years ago, too narrow now, but with a lot of 'dead' street during the afternoon. Can we agree that the afternoon of the murder was the probable time, if the supposition is valid, reasons being:—

1. Old Mrs Cream and Miss Birch would be asleep.

2. Rumming, the cook, was watching the TV, probably half cut.

3. The time factor meant that you ideally did not want the substitute spear hanging around too long.

"Now, there is one more thing, but one minute." The Commander dialled a number and spoke for ten minutes.

"That was the chairman of the hotel group," he said. "I happen to know him. Fortunately, as Grädde apparently has a sizeable wad of their shares. He has maintained this suite there fourteen years, since the place was built. There is a chauffeur, a Cockney, who drives Grädde when he is here and is content to accept board wages when his master is abroad. In the suite, which consists of eight rooms, sleep an old Swedish valet who has been with Grädde for forty years, and a young Swedish secretary. As in all hotels the front of the house masks considerable activity behind. Goods and staff lifts, back staircases etcetera. It is possible that over all those years Grädde would be familiar with all this. Sometimes, in these days, very important people prefer to duck through the staff warrens rather than try to get through the foyer and the TV cameras. That is that.

"The last point is that the workmanship of the duplicate spear is professional: I use the term to distinguish it from a high-class handyman job. Herr Grädde was trained in the way we higher breeds disdain. To prepare for his inheritance he not only went through the shops, but took a degree and acted as a manager. He was thirty when he got his first executive job in charge of the Berlin office. This comes, reluctantly, from the Foreign Office. He could get a job as a toolmaker any day."

"I still don't think you have much," said Treasury Counsel. "I mean it sounds good in here, but if you got a good, or half good man against you he'd cut it to ribbons. I'd like a few facts, sir, of the kind juries accept. 'When the chain's swinging the seat's warm', that's the logic that juries understand."

"Gentlemen of the Jerry, in fact," said a wag.

"You might call them that," said Counsel, grimly, "but bury them in facts!"

"The time factor is the thing we must clear," said the Commander dismally, wondering whether this Bermuda caper was all it was cracked up to be. Somebody had told him you had to have three thousand pounds a year clear which, by dint of some shifty work regarding his wife's marriage settlement he might manage to raise, take or more likely give a few hundred. He didn't like this business at all, and Sir John had got in the wrong plane scheduled for Miami from Kingsford Smith Airport. On the way it had been hijacked and Sir John was now in Havana with little prospect of immediate return to anywhere. The poor fellow had always had a bad travel record. Shipwrecked, hadn't he been, the Commander remembered, then saw that everyone was waiting. The trouble was that you had to say something, not like that bloody fellow Reed seated there with his fat chops relaxed and hands across his belly. As a matter of course, his face had assumed an expression of deep thought.

"The only two points I have is that on the Monday, the day on which the alleged crime occurred, room service was abnormally preoccupied with the Grädde suite. For reasons which we know, the substitution occurred around two, possibly three, when the ladies were sleeping or watching TV, and, we'll say, ten at the outside when no outsider could safely be inside. Every hour, Grädde had room service. Oh, drinks—he confined himself to coffee, but twice about minor complaints, once the plumbing, the other about noise in the corridor made by the chambermaids—he got the assistant manager for those. Abnormality. Usually the factotum or the secretary makes coffee or serves snacks from the refrigerators. However he could only have made it to and from the Cream house by means of transport. Thanks to the chairman I got the facts regarding hotel service this morning. Whichever way you look at it Grädde had an hour to cover a return journey of ten miles which means transport."

"Why did he leave the bike there, I wonder?" said Quant.

Reed was feeling loquacious and devil-may-care. "First the lock, Commander, to the door of the old storeroom. It's a very fair job, but a man of Herr Grädde's craftsmanship would make very little weather of it. He must have a workshop somewhere, probably a string of them. Who is better entitled to have a home workshop than an armament magnate?"

"Keep to the point, Sergeant," said the Commander.

"Cycling one way, walking hurriedly the other, he could have done it. The obvious reason he ditched the bike is that it had a puncture. After all those years the inner tubes would about be useless. He would have wheeled it out of the yard, pumped tyres up the day before. But in his methodical way he never imagined that anybody would have a bike with rotten inner tubes. At Larchmont he took the precaution of bringing the bike in. What the hell? If anybody saw him he was only Mr Grädde with the eccentric wish to cycle through London because of his liver trouble. He had no patching material to mend the tube, even if (a) he had the time; or (b) the rotten rubber would take a patch. So he trusted to his legs."

"Did he not take a risk?" asked Quant, slowly, reluctant as it were to wager a life peerage upon Grädde's guilt.

"I think," said Treasury Counsel, "that even if anybody saw him coming out of Larchmont, a jury would not believe him guilty beyond benefit of reasonable doubt. But have you thought," he hesitated, "of the divorce between

Hans Grädde and Mrs Cream. From the papers he seems to have been a man with very queer streaks. I mean, eating smoked fish in bed with his popsy"—he was, the Commander noted, rather young for his position in life—"but suppose he did not actually divorce Hezekiah Cream. I take it her Swedish was probably rudimentary."

"Good God," said the Commander.

"Generally," said Counsel, "she would have difficulty in proceeding. And it very much depends upon Swedish law. However you realise that there must have been an element of fraud. You will find that Sven-Eric, when he knew the position, or perhaps his mother, spent a lot of time squaring people. That means the Grädde inheritance was obtained by Sven-Eric, knowingly or not, by fraud and it simply cannot stand. It is purely a supposition."

The Commander, who was not particularly keen on going home that night, promptly telephoned for an open return to Stockholm and his emergency suitcase.

"The Swedes, thank God," he told the others, "mostly speak better English than we do. I leave in one hour. Pray take my chair, Mr Quant."

Sourly watched by the old Super, who had been vaguely planning a crash call to Gibraltar to investigate the contamination of the natives from over the Spanish border, the Commander left.

"Well," Quant said at last after portentously moving his notebooks upon the small dais, and getting some satisfaction from the looks of two gentlemen, equal in rank, who resented it.

"We might be able to close the file," he said, "if the supposition is correct. I can think of no greater incentive to murder. The earlier death of Peter Cream, with its possible mechanical trap, would point a finger to Grädde. A man who owns a sizeable chunk of Europe by any reasonable standard, stripped of his possessions . . . Ach."

"Even if stripped," suggested an Envious Equal, "his directorship would be worth many times what I earn. I looked him up : on the board of seventeen companies."

"When the market falls you cannot sell," said Quant, "yourself or your shares. Oh, no doubt, a sinecure would be found, but to a man accustomed to power of any sort . . . You well know that a lot of top financial embezzlement has precisely the same motivation. We have the following : a grease gun; a workshop where he may have fashioned the spear; anybody who may have relevantly seen him. What do you want to say, Mr Reed?"

"I only glimpsed the factotum. The secretary is a pallid chap, hyper-efficient one would say, and I have no doubt that Grädde owns him body and soul. If you like we— Jarvis and I—might try the chauffeur. But the particular point is that when Grädde entered the house on the night of the murder—supposedly driven by the usual bad nerves a murderer gets after the kill—he was wearing very flashy clothing. Assuming he wore old clothes to match the bike, he might have thought out the disguise-in-reverse stunt, in which you wear not only the direct opposite, but something so flashy that it takes the watcher's attention completely off your face or idiosyncracies of carriage."

"You have a lot there," said Quant. "He was dressed flashy. I mean for a gentleman on the directorship of the International Bank."

"You mean he should look like an undertaker?" suggested the wag.

"Why not perhaps like an unsuccessful comedian," capped Counsel.

"Or a kind of philanthropic male madam giving credit to the penniless johns," said an old inspector.

"He did not look like the director of the International Bank," said Quant with suitable firmness. "I think, Mr Reed, that you might well try to wheedle the chauffeur, or at any rate try to establish some line of communication which might be broadened. Do you know who he is?"

"I'll find him," said Reed and went out to the nearest pub.

It was routine to find the chauffeur. Reed left it to Sergeant Jarvis who in turn approached the hotel functionary who dealt among other things with private servants frequenting the premises. There was a waiting room for such people, though Grädde's arrangement was that the man phoned in every day at one-fifteen, the car being often parked in his own small garage two miles away.

The chauffeur was a hypochondriac, the functionary had said, and so he proved, a dapper man found in the waiting room of Dr. Ley, a Chinese herbalist then in vogue.

The waiting room was full, both with people and illustrated but rather strange charts of the human body.

Jarvis, a detailed description of the man in his mind, went into action. "If you'll excuse me, sir," he said huskily, "but I saw you come in. Is it the back, sir, because it's my first time here, and yours looked as though it hurt cruelly when you went up the stairs?"

"It's shoulders, too," whined the chauffeur. "It creeps up along the spine. He's given me powdered elephants' tusks and dried lizards and it does relieve it. He now proposes to make liddle tiny fires of gunpower to arouse the nerves. There's a petition to get it on the National Health, the doctors not being any good."

"Ah," said Jarvis, warning off Reed with his eyes. "I do feel like a good health drink of chlorophyll, if they have them around here. I mean the real green stuff."

"That's a curious thing," said the chauffeur, "on account of my brother having a health bar up the street,

176

along with selling vegetarian delicacies. He invented the well-known asparagus and spinach extract, the same having a curious and beneficial effect upon the water. He also has a purge made from prickly pear, imported from Australia, which can only be described as spectacular : just take half a cupful and be sure the loo is not bespoke."

"Looks as though we might be waiting a long time," groaned Jarvis, massaging the small of his back.

"Have you been cast?" asked the chauffeur.

"Cast?"

"He must have your horoscope. He can't even start before that. I might mention, sir, that if you can remember the details—he likes the exact time as far as it can be remembered—my brother casts them effortlessly. Perhaps we might indulge in a healing beverage while he does the job. Eight pounds ten, sir, and it's hand written—no typing—on genuine imitation parchment with the signs of the Zodiac printed in four colours. One cannot get fairer than that."

"Could he make it eight pounds . . . ? The money I've paid out on my back is something cruel."

The chauffeur pursed his lips. "I might use my influence beneficially, I'm sure, but of course it has to be cash. Once he discovered that the client was going to die within half an hour and the bloke had no ready cash on him."

"Did he?" asked Jarvis, genuinely interested.

"He never came back," said the chauffeur, "and the cheque was dishonoured. Perhaps we might slip round to the brother, sir."

After a discreet twenty minutes, Reed followed, enquiring of a man whose life's work seemed to be digging a large hole in the road.

"The health shop is down a 'undred yards on the right. 'Aescalapius' it's called. I tell you quite straight, mate, that if it's poisoning yer guts you're after, that's the right shop, so help me, and I've been digging here for the last eight years. The brews they sell first take you short, then begin to gripe and put you to bed with auntie biotics for a solid week. There's a good old English pub a bit away from it. Be a man, sir, and have some healthy English ale with perhaps a drop of gin as a tightener." He returned to his leisurely use of the shovel.

Good Lord! thought poor Reed, racking his brains; suddenly like a revelation he thought of tomato juice. You were safe with the stuff, thanks to Heinz, a bland, unalterable brew from tin or bottle. He perked up and slid on to a stool to one side of the chauffeur whose brother could be dimly sighted in a glass cubicle, books around him evidently preparing Jarvis's horoscope.

A sly young lady poured juice from a jug into a glass embellished with a stencil of Tarzan.

Small beads of sweat stood out on his forehead after the first swig.

"The first taste does startle you, luv," said the young lady with malice. "All the juice is home made. Have you tried the chlorophyll and carrot, ducks? You don't smell and you can see in the dark. It's very popular with gentlemen."

Reed got his morning paper out of his pocket and read the sporting news again.

"I'm in the insurance business," Jarvis was whining, "which is hard on the back because of you having to bow and scrape all the blessed time. But for disloyalty to the company, I'd wish some of the ladies collected their security before the figures tell us they should."

The insurance agent persona was one which readily covered a multitude of sins and most detectives became adept at it. Reed noticed that even the Sergeant could not help but betray a slight nervousness as he sipped whatever health fluid it was that the chauffeur had talked him into.

It was Jarvis at his best. Soon he and the chauffeur were talking in low, confidential tones. Reed paid for his juice, standing on the counter minus one sip, and went in search of the pub. It was a cosy one, and he settled down with a pint and was on his second, three-quarters of an hour later, when the saloon door opened and Jarvis peered in.

"Thought I'd find you here," he said as he flopped down in a chair. "And for the first time in years I shall break my gait and have a brandy."

"Take my advice and have a drop of port mixed with it," said Reed and went to order.

Jarvis drank half at a gulp.

"Did you get your eight quid horoscope?" leered Reed.

Jarvis glared and tapped a pocket. "Though how *that'll* look on expenses God knows." He brightened. "He says I'm coming into money. Do you think there's anything to it?"

"God knows." Reed felt a trifle queasy as the juice repeated. "What did you get?"

"One thing. The chauffeur was due for a day off, the day on which Giles Cream was killed. He was under instructions when he was working to telephone for instructions at 1.15. Grädde's secretary, or very occasionally his man-of-all-work, used to answer and tell him what the master wished. There was no reply. Grädde had a direct outside line, but the chauffeur got the reception desk and sure enough the suite was not answering. He was just going to try in ten minutes' time when he remembered that it was a day off for him. My assumption is that Grädde gave his whole staff the day off. The chauffeur—he was getting a little suspicious of me by then—did say that he sometimes waited with his car in the loading yard in the early afternoon when it's deserted and Grädde used to come down in the service lift. They had management permission and it is congested at the front of the place."

"I think we'll go back and put it on Quant's dinner plate," said Reed slowly.

179

His colleague, who was looking a little green, winced at the word 'dinner' but nodded assent.

They found Quant in his office staring dismally at a map of Gibraltar and an advertisement for a bullfight in La Linea.

"Well?"

Of the two of them Jarvis was the better reporter, but without being asked he had seated himself and was mopping his forehead.

"I think I'd better go home, sir, on account of feeling sick."

The old Super was always interested in matters of health.

"Would ye like a nice cooling fruit drink before you go?"

Jarvis crammed a handkerchief to his mouth and departed at once.

"Something he ate, no doubt," said Quant, massaging his jaw. "Now, Sergeant, between us I have very disturbing news. The Commander is just completing his journey, but I had a visit from Mr Ambrose Cream, a very smart man is that, with both eyes on the main chance. He has gone through the scanty family records that remain and suggested that old Hans Grädde never in fact divorced old Mrs Cream, as indeed we already suspect."

"Gawd," said Reed. "I thought, I mean I hardly believed it."

"I had Grädde's wedding looked up. About the time Cream's boy was born, he was in Scotland marrying a Duke's daughter at a church. I suppose it was one of the few times he came out during the day."

"Seems a strange alliance."

"She was not young, the family had had reverses, the more sensational papers said the marriage settlement was to be two hundred thousand. Hmph."

"But would not somebody know?"

"According to Ambrose old Grädde never announced

either his marriage or his divorce, or so the old lady says. She is naturally upset."

"A wonderful motive for murder I suppose Giles knew."

"I think he may have found out, as Peter may have before. He had some small business interests in Sweden: perhaps a day there with little to do and an enquiring mind took over. Well, you'd better attend the noon conference tomorrow. And there's a job for you. See what you can find out about these two men that Grädde employs. I doubt whether it will be much, they'll be chosen for the fact they can keep their traps shut."

Reed chose to have a word with the Hotel Squad in the shape of a middle-aged man, handsome but not too handsome (with the type of face you cannot easily recognise again), and excellent, medium-priced clothes. He and his fellows stood at hotel bars, dined in the restaurants, stood filling in long documents at reception desks, and between them could remember the faces of some two thousand hotel thieves.

"Grädde, eh," said the handsome man. "The Cream case, I suppose. He has kept on that suite for years: a shareholder, too, one believes. I've only seen him. Funny devil, sleeps all the morning they say. It'll be difficult, but I do have a friend there. Sit down for five minutes."

It in fact took him nearly a quarter of an hour and some persuasive talking.

"It appears," he said, "Herr Grädde is not reckoned a chap to be meddled with. Anyway, the valet or what-have-you, is a sour, tall fellow, in his seventies. He hardly ever goes out and it is impossible to make any conversation with him. The secretary is a different kettle of fish. Pleasant in a very neutral way, willing to exchange generalisations. At this hour he always has his lunch in a small sit-at-the-counter salad and hors-d'oeuvre bar at the hotel. It's favoured by weight-watchers. You can try your luck. Grädde went out three-quarters of an hour ago, at one o'clock."

He seemed doomed to the health-food path, thought

Reed as he entered the Salad Bar, a place carefully tricked out in warm colours that made you look healthy. He was in no hurry and collected a small tuna salad and white coffee. Most of the tables were singles or doubles. People, most of them showing signs of being in a hurry, gobbled up salad and walked out. In the corner furthest from him he watched the pale-faced male secretary, eyes hidden behind glasses, take a second serving, then afterwards select a portion of pie and cream and a second coffee. Reed supposed he liked the stuff. He pushed away his half-finished plate and walked over.

"I'm fearfully sorry to interrupt your lunch, sir, but my name is Sergeant Reed of the Criminal Investigation Department. I was looking for Herr Grädde, but he is apparently out."

"He will be in conference until seven tonight." The young man was a cool card, thought Reed.

"You know how we policemen have to get every little point sewn up."

"On the contrary, I know nothing of police procedure." There was an accent, a suggestion of pendantry, but very little.

"On Monday, the day before Mr. Cream died, sir, we just require details of Mr Grädde's movements."

"I cannot in any circumstance discuss my employer."

"Oh, I suppose you were in the suite with him all day, sir, no harm in confirming *that*."

"I think you must approach Herr Grädde."

"Been with him long, sir?" In police work you learned to be unabashed.

"Five years." The secretary gave a thin smile, but his voice remained pleasant enough. "And, you see, I would prefer to be with him another five. It is a very good job indeed and may one day lead to a better one."

Reed thanked him, phoned in a report, and went home very early.

CHAPTER NINE

At next morning's conference, Reed thought that
he had never seen the Commander look worse. Great bags
floated under the protuberant eyes, the neat pepper and
salt moustache managed to look scrubby and even false. He
supposed he had not had any sleep.

Though he purchased his suits at reasonable tailors,
Quant, on the other hand, managed to look like a healthy
Victorian parson out on an anonymous spree.

"Gentlemen," said the Commander, "to sum up. Hans
Grädde made a will in due form six months before his
death. It left 'fifty per cent of my possessions outright to
my son or his heirs; fifty per cent of my possessions to my
grandchildren or their heirs the said possessions to be sold
at the discretion of my executors and the sum divided
among them after thirty years has elapsed from my
death.' "

He sighed. "That is the translation of the Swedish. His
wife predeceased him. She left most of her money back to
the ducal family whence she came, having as it were done
her duty. One of Grädde's peculiarities was an increasing
reluctance to sign anything. He was tottery for two years
before his death and no basis could be found for a compar-
ison of signature. So the will could have been forged—
witnesses now dead, the private secretary who presumably
typed it, the same."

"I do not see why Sven-Eric Grädde should have forged
it," observed Quant.

"The old man might have died intestate and that would
have caused an enquiry to establish exactly what heirs he
had, which would doubtless have incurred newspaper

publicity. And if Sven-Eric *had* forged it he might have
been too cunning and cautious to give the name of the
son his father was referring to. I think that there is a
strong presumption that Sven-Eric knew the position at the
time of his father's death. He did not get on too well with
the old man, who was a malicious, eccentric old brute, or
so I was told. Now as to the business of Mrs Cream,
there is a copy of the wedding certificate—it was a civil
ceremony: but no such registration of divorce exists
between that date and the date of his second marriage.
Then I got three bloody lawyers haranguing me at our
embassy.

"It seems that Sven-Eric would plead that the marriage
was irregular in the first place. Secondly, Mrs Cream had
abandoned any claim to have legally married Hans
Grädde. A parent cannot bastardise his child, but Mrs
Cream's son is long since dead and made no attempt in his
lifetime to claim his inheritance. It is in any case a tricky
point."

"The son did not know about it," protested Quant.

"And how do you prove that?" asked the Commander
impatiently. "I tell you a dozen lawyers will buy small
estates out of this one unless it is arbitrated. Before I left
for the plane home, I had a double Scotch—and God, did
I need one—with the most human of the lawyers. I put a
question to him man-to-man, and he said, off the record,
that the Creams can take Sven-Eric's coat and hat, always
providing that old Mrs Cream will co-operate.

"So it now seems to me that the balance of probabilities
are overwhelmingly for Sven-Eric having murdered Giles
Cream. It will take weeks of mass interviewing, unless
we're lucky, to find somebody who saw him leaving or
coming back to the hotel. However, I have the highest
authority for mass interviewing and," he smiled nastily,
"hang Mr Sven-Eric Grädde and his influence."

Reed got up. "I'm afraid you'll find that the manservant

184

and the secretary will swear that one or the other of them had him in sight at all relevant times."

"We know he gave them the afternoon off," said Quant. "Your report and another made it clear. Grädde sent them out, attempted to establish an alibi by summoning a member of the hotel staff on each hour."

"We cannot prove that they were not in the suite when waiters etcetera came in : it's a big suite. And if somebody saw them go out, well they'd just swear it was on a five minute errand."

"There is the chauffeur and the unanswered phone calls."

"A lot of people, feeling in a certain mood, let the thing ring. A friend of mine keeps his inside a cupboard for that purpose. I'm afraid that a junior could tie that chauffeur into knots at will—the man drinks spinach juice!"

"And you think the secretary and the servant would lie to save their master?" asked the Commander, thinking of the joy his own would experience in *not* throwing a life-belt.

"I think the manservant is the type of old and faithful servitor who would cut his arm off for Grädde. The secretary is a polite young smoothy with ambition. At this moment, Grädde could sign a cheque for a hundred thousand with no difficulty . . . I doubt whether we can get enough to convince a jury."

"Hrmph," said the Commander. "When she hears that Grädde is suspected of murdering her grandson—and very possibly Peter as well—Mrs Cream will surely become vindictive and fight on our side. We'd need her to get the motive into the evidence. And a damned powerful motive it is. One always thinks that an English jury is a bit incredulous of jealousy, but grips on to money like a bulldog. This needs blue-printing, but you get on with the old lady, Sergeant—get a car out to Larchmont. I don't have to dot the i's with you. Hint that Grädde might be the murderer.

185

Don't bother her with a notebook, indent for a tape. We do not want a statement at this juncture, just a good idea of what she might give."

Reed happily went out. He had no intention of getting himself into some mammoth, metatarsal-flattening project by which every inhabitant of a large area of north London was interrogated as to whether they had seen Mr Grädde at the relevant time. He signed a small, expensive recorder out. It was concealed in a broad black trouser belt and could record up to three hours. He was badly delayed by the traffic and it was just after two when he approached Larchmont.

Impelled by a policeman's sixth sense, Reed drove round the block at snail's pace.

He thought he recognised Dick Cream's Jaguar and—he whistled and turned his head—wiping the windscreen of a small Bentley was Grädde's chauffeur.

He drove on half a mile and went into a pub and got a half of bitter. Presently he borrowed the telephone on the counter. The Commander was in Whitehall and must not be interrupted. Quant was out, as was his deputy. Everybody seemed out. The Sergeant did not like it at all. Coldly assessing it, he did not think the Commander would hesitate in putting him before a retirement board, neither did he think that the board would hesitate in recommending it. He shrugged and drove back to Larchmont. The front door took some seconds to open, perhaps even a minute.

"Do you intend haunting this place at meal times?" Ambrose was looking at his most unpleasant.

"There is a certain form you can get at any local station, sir, for the submission of complaints. I wish to see your grandmother. If necessary I can get a warrant to enter this house. I dare say the press would get wind of it and we would prefer not to have the publicity."

It was an approach which nearly always worked with businessmen. 'Publish and be damned' is a fine, bold phrase, but when it comes to the point people do not make use of it; Ambrose, therefore, looked sour and stood back from the door.

"I am at a conference in the dining room," he said. "Mrs Cream's in her sitting room. I don't imagine you have forgotten the way."

"No, sir," said the Sergeant stolidly and walked down the corridor to the room at the end, where Mrs Cream, on her red plush throne, was drinking champagne and eating chicken sandwiches.

"Hallo, it's the pleasant policeman," she said. "As you see the children gave Rumming and Miss Birch the day off. They are having a conference."

"All of them plus Mr Grädde, eh?"

"That's right. The whisky is on the sideboard, by the way."

Presently Reed sat sipping and peering up at her. The drapes were half drawn and the room was very dark.

"You know, Mrs Grädde . . ." he said.

"It's Cream, stupid fellow!"

"Hans Grädde got no divorce: if so it's not on record. Your wedding was, but not the divorce."

"What a clown he was in some ways." The old lady still preserved a dimple when she laughed.

"It was Sweden, I suppose, where he got it?" asked the Sergeant. "I mean you didn't get a mail order job from Mexico?"

"I don't think they had 'em in those days," said the old lady. "No, he said it was Sweden, and it was their writing I saw when I signed. But, good heavens. It must be a mistake." A thought struck her and she chuckled. "He did have a peculiar sense of humour, you know. However, it doesn't matter."

"It might matter a good deal to the Grädde family. If

you will forgive me saying so—quite impertinently—the Gräddes are both acquisitive and determined."

"Oh, I quite admit that. Somehow the quality missed my son who was charming but feckless, but it has been inherited by Sven-Eric and all my grandchildren."

"Has it occurred to you that the deaths of Giles and Peter may have been because they had discovered that the present Gräddes possessed money which should be theirs? Suppose Hans, in his delightful manner, had chuckled and said to himself, 'let them fight it out and the best man win'."

"That was his philosophy to a tee, but what exactly are you getting at?"

"Just thinking aloud."

"I am not sure that I appreciate it."

"You know, Mrs Cream, police work is not very nice work. The stench of it makes the public recoil when they themselves get near to crime, such as murder. That's part of our trouble—to persuade members of the public to open their eyes and help us rather than shutting 'em. Only the criminals benefit from the latter, I assure you." Reed got up. "I'll be back to say goodbye after I have dropped into the dining room."

The door was thick and the keyhole had a little draught-preventing flap on each side—a Victorian refinement. Checking the fact that his tape recorder was in 'on' position still, Reed perfunctorily tapped and opened the door.

At the head of the dining room table sat Ambrose Cream, on his left his sister Joan, on his right Sally and Dick. Facing him was Sven-Eric Grädde.

"Get out!" Blood suffused Ambrose's normally pale cheekbones.

"If I get out I go to the local police station, but *you accompany me for questioning.*"

"About what?" Joan Cream was placatory.

"The fact that the late Hans Grädde was never divorced from your grandmother."

In spite of himself there was momentary triumph upon Ambrose's thin face. The others looked at him.

Grädde was as urbane as ever. "Ambrose suggested this half an hour ago. I replied that I had never heard of it. There would be difficulties of proof : everybody connected with it would of course be dead after these long years."

"It was not checked when your father's will was proven?"

"I take it that nobody ever imagined any check was necessary. My father and mother had married with some, uh, international publicity. Nobody in Sweden would have called him a bigamist. I imagine there is some simple explanation : an official record lost or," he lowered his voice, "stolen."

"One trusts you do not believe that our family have been getting off with Swedish records?" Sally Cream was contemptuous.

"Good Lord, no, Sally. It is a fact that my father had a genius, more than that, a delight, in making enemies. Somebody might have concocted an original revenge. However, we shall, as I have said before, come to some settlement or else go to law, and a protracted case it would be, with, I imagine, no precedents."

"Mr Grädde," snapped Reed out of the blue, "why did you ride here on a bicycle between one and two last Monday, the day of the murder, and let yourself into the house when you knew that nobody would be around?"

"That is absurd," said Grädde.

Reed remained silent. A few minutes before his trained eye had seen a hatch in one corner of the room. A servery from the kitchen, he concluded, but as he looked the oaken panel had almost imperceptibly slid back a couple of inches. It half distracted his attention.

"Are you accusing Herr Grädde of murder?" asked Dick.

189

"If I were I would have to give him various warnings. I think he might have certain information it is his duty to divulge."

In Grädde's face was something which could have been the faint, leering reflection of inward triumph. Of course, thought the Sergeant, a man of such resource, a man whose business was often wrapped in secrecy, might be an adept at simple disguise. A reddish wig, a little padding inside the cheeks, adjustable, if you had practised, in a matter of seconds. It might make their task impossible.

"We would not want Grandma troubled with all this," said Dick Cream, uneasily.

"It is for the sake of the grand old lady," said Sven-Eric in tones of sanctimony, "that I will give a short statement. During that day I never left my hotel, and at no time was for more than ten minutes away from either the secretary or my valet. I was engaged on banking matters of great international importance. I made a call to a very important person at 1.25."

From the call box a hundred yards from Larchmont, thought Reed grimly, but unprovable.

He sighed and got up, noticing that the hatch was now closed.

"Thank you. Don't worry, I'll let myself out." He saw Ambrose hesitate, then nod curtly. Reed guessed that he did not want to leave the others at a crucial point. The Sergeant therefore made his way to the kitchen, noting that Mrs Rumming had left it scrupulously clean. The hatchway was next to the Aga cooker. Gingerly he slid it open an inch.

"... no need to get at cross purposes," he heard Grädde's voice saying. "You must decide whether going to law would benefit you. I can promise you that it would drive you mad and hamper your creative drive for some years perhaps. But our men of business can work out a compromise : and of course I should have no objection to deepening our business association. Perhaps we might even look at the United States."

"Well, Sven-Eric," said Ambrose, "I wonder whether you could leave us for an hour: you could sit with Grandma who is very fond of you in her way."

"I understand. In an hour, then."

"What do we do?" asked Sally as the door closed.

"I think he's right. We gouge the most out of him we can, bearing in mind that the creative side is what primarily interests us. With money we can be the biggest as well as best," said Joan Cream, her voice a little shrill.

Reed went out of the kitchen carefully and walked to the closed door of the drawing room. He had one hand outstretched to knock when he heard the single staccato rap of a small gun. Twisting the knob he rushed through. Herr Grädde was sprawled on the red carpet, the small hole in the centre of his forehead telling the story. He died before the Sergeant could turn his eyes up to Mrs Cream's throne, where the old lady sat with an old-fashioned target pistol in her right hand.

Reed turned and twisted the key in the lock of the door. Turning to the telephone he dialled Emergency, and ordered an ambulance and then police.

"Hans gave me this because he knew I liked to shoot. He would have been amused. Oh, I kept it because I lived alone. It was in that cabinet with a lot of old things." She nodded to an elegant Edwardian cupboard.

"You heard through the hatch in the kitchen?"

"I heard," she said. "I know the Gräddes. You would never have proved it. I remembered, too, that he was in England when my poor Peter died."

"Listen to me, Mrs Cream. I saw it. You had been showing him some old mementoes which you had been sitting up there examining. Without your knowing it the gun was loaded. As you picked it up it went off. I saw it, remember! And that's all you say."

"As a family we can always remember our lines," said Mrs Cream with slight bitterness. "But why are you doing this?"

"As a tribute to your late husband's sense of humour, perhaps."

There was a pounding at the door.

"What's the matter?" shouted Ambrose Cream.

"A slight accident," answered the Sergeant and turned the key.